Born in Monaghan in 1907, Michael McLaverty was educated in Belfast and London. He became a schoolteacher in Belfast and was later a headmaster there until his retirement. *Lost Fields* is the second of his eight novels which Poolbeg Press is re-issuing, his *Collected Short Stories* and first novel, *Call My Brother Back*, having already appeared.

Lost Fields

MICHAEL McLAVERTY

poolbeg press

First published 1942 by
Jonathan Cape Ltd.,

This edition published 1980 by
Poolbeg Press Ltd.,
Knocksedan House,
Swords, Co. Dublin, Ireland.

© Michael McLaverty 1980

The generous assistance of the Arts Council of Northern
Ireland in the publication of this book is gratefully acknow-
ledged.

Designed by Steven Hope
Cover by Robert Ballagh

Printed by Cahill Printers Limited,
East Wall Road, Dublin 3.

Chapter I

The air in the kitchen was heavy and stale; it clung to the coats that quietly hung from the doors, brooded in the corners, and lay like a hood over the cold black fireplace. Outside it was raining and handfuls of it were wind-flung against the window. As dawn approached a dull light squeezed through the yellow blind; the shadows shrank from the corners and the hood lifted from the fireplace.

A lark's cage hung close to the window and the lark itself stretched its wings and sharpened its bill on the wires of the cage. It yawned, flicked its wings, and husks of seed fell noiselessly on to the red tiles of the kitchen floor. The light brightened and the horizontal sash of the window was outlined on the blind. The red-distempered walls glowed, and on a string across the fireplace could be seen a pair of green socks and baby's clothes. A man's collar with the tie still in it hung over a picture of St. Patrick. and under a sunken sofa were children's boots with stockings stuffed into their tops. The fire was dead out and close to the shining fender was a rocking-chair with the seat of it mended by criss-crossed cord.

Presently someone moved in the wee room off the kitchen, and the lark chirped twice when he saw the door open and Mary Griffin come into the kitchen. She was about twenty, but looked more. She had a pale, sad face, black hair, and in her left ear a piece of wadding. There was nothing alive about her except her hands which moved gracefully as she turned the tap in the scullery, washed her face, and rhythmically rolled her plaits into a bun. She took the man's collar and put it in the chest of drawers, went to the red lamp that burned before a picture of the Sacred Heart and pinched the almost-deadened wick with a forefinger and thumb. By the clock on the mantelpiece she saw it was half-six; so she took the brush, and from under the chest of drawers retrieved two glass marbles, a brass cogged wheel with a string on it, and a mouth-organ with no teeth. Quietly she raked the ashes and prepared the fire.

She touched the blind and it flew from her hands the tassel striking the top pane of the window. With a hand to her mouth she listened rigidly, but there was no sound from upstairs and going to the front door she let herself out and moved almost on tip-toe down the wet street.

The mist gradually faded from the corners of the window and there could be seen the closed doors on the opposite side and a cat sheltering on one of the window-sills. The rain streaked the red brick under the eaves and fell pattering on a sodden newspaper that stuck to the wet road. Drops formed on the arms of the lamp-posts and were quickly blown off again. Holes in the street filled up with rain-water and when the wind rippled across them it made waves as tiny as the markings on a bird's wing.

The lark hopped excitedly on its sod of grass. A man came downstairs in his bare feet, boots in one hand, a cup in the other, and his braces trailing across the floor.

'Good God, this is a country and a half! Rain again! 'Tis a wonder we haven't webbed feet!'

He cracked his fingers at the lark: 'Give us a bit of a song a morning like that and don't always be looking for grub.'

He pressed his thumb into the sole of his boot and then searched in the coal-hole for a piece of cardboard, and finally when he had his boots on he discovered a hole in the heel of his sock and smudged it over with ashes. He peeped into the wee room: 'I don't know, under God, how she rises for Mass a morning like that. And what with all the praying you'd think we'd have better luck.'

He went to the stairs and kicked them with the

6

assurance of a man who had been up since cock-crow.

'Heigh!' he shouted, 'are ye going to sleep the whole day? Katie, get up! Heigh, Kate, it's time the childer were on the road to school.' He turned from the stairs muttering to himself: 'Ye can't get them to bed at night and only hunger drives them out of it in the morning.'

From the cage he took the seed-trough, blowing the husks into the fire, and shaking up the fresh seed from the bottom. He pulled his braces over his shoulders and stamped about to ease his feet. Fresh water he gave to the lark and then went out by the back door to cut a sod for it.

While he was out, Katie, his wife, came down the stairs. She wore a black blouse with a chain of safety pins dangling from it and on her feet a pair of slippers wrinkled at the heels. Her head was thrust forward in an attitude of fussy haste, but unlike her daughter she was clumsy in her movements, trying to do too many things at once, dropping spoons and tripping rashly over the bag that served as a mat near the scullery door.

'Somebody will break their neck on that and it'll not be me,' and she lifted the bag and flung it behind the coal-hole door. 'Just another of his fol-de-lols, and if he'd use it a body wouldn't mind. He'd still have the iron mat he found at the dumps only the dog trapped his paw in it.'

With difficulty she stopped and pulled out a boy's boot from below the sofa. The sole was hanging off. 'Just as I thought — well, he'll bend his back and mend it before I do it.'

She got up with a groan, placed enamel mugs on the table and a saucer with butter to melt on the hob. From a jug on the shelf she took her purse and emptied out four pennies into the palm of her hand and gazed at them reproachfully. In the wee room she began counting the handkerchiefs which

7

Mary had hemmed, and when she heard the latch lift on the scullery door she came out and saw Johnny with a slushy sod in his hand. A greyhound with straw sticking to its coat rushed in and lay under the sofa.

'Ye think more about that lark than you do about the children ... Didn't I tell you to tack on the sole of Frankie's boot. And look at it there and it hanging off.'

'Rain outside and a storm inside. This is no country for any Christian.'

'Quit the preaching,' she interrupted, 'and bend your back and tack on the sole. 'Deed I suppose I'll have to do it myself.'

'Sure there's plenty of time, bags of time,' he added, the wet sod dreeping on to the floor. 'I'll wallop it on with two smacks from the hammer. Hould yer whisht for a minute or two.'

'There'd be nothing done in this house unless I rhyme and rhyme. I'm sick, sore, and tired of it. And there's the wooden legs of the bed you were to shorten before your mother comes. How could an ould woman climb into that bed without a step-ladder?'

Johnny had got the last from below the sofa and was already working the boy's boot on to it.

'Are you going to nag about the old woman again?' he answered her. 'Haven't I worn out a pair of pants cycling down to her? And look at the shine in the seat of these ones — you could shave in them.'

'Well, John Joseph, it's a poor lookout for us if she doesn't come. You haven't got a job with your barrow for the past two weeks, and her pension would clear the boards for us. Ye can't keep the door shut on the rent man all the time. Go down to her again, Johnny, in God's name. Tell her she'll have a room and a bed to herself and all her orders. What'd she say the last time?'

With stiff deliberation he rested the hammer on

the sole of the boot, folded his arms, and looked up at her with an expression of absolute patience.

'Do you want me to go over all that again? She said that the smoke of the city would kill her and the noise of the traffic would put her cracked. "I'm better where I am — the chapel a few fields away, my hens about the door, and my independence" . . . That's the whole story,' and he lifted the hammer again and whacked at the sole.

'You didn't frighten her enough,' Kate assured him. 'What if she fell, or something happened her during the night and her nearest neighbour a quarter of a mile away?'

'I told her all that. But she talks as much about her independence as all our Irish leaders rolled into one.' He hit his thumb with the hammer, and shook it in the air. 'Will you give over talking to me while I'm working?' he shouted angrily.

She laughed ironically: 'It's well seen a hammer and you are not old friends.'

Frankie Griffin, a boy of eleven, came jumping down the stairs, his trousers patched, and sleep still in his eyes. He looked at the clock, at the table, and at his father bent over the last.

'Where's Peter?' his mother asked him.

'He's sick!' and he turned down the neck of his shirt in a V.

Kate rushed up the stairs and went into the back room. There were two beds in it. In the big bed Peter, a black-haired boy of fifteen, had the clothes tucked up under his chin.

'What ails you?' she asked breathlessly.

'I'm sick,' and he half-shut his eyes.

'Where are you sick?'

'There!' making a limp gesture towards his stomach.

She leaned over the bed and felt his head: 'Now put out your tongue!'

She winked an eye and pursed her lips: 'Put on

9

yourself and get to your school before I take the belt to you!' She took his trousers from the knob of the bed and threw them over him. 'Jump into them, this minute, and none of your capers.'

When she came down the child had heard her voice, and from upstairs he began to howl, and she sent Frankie up to him. He took the stairs two at a time and carried down the child and strapped him into a chair which had a semicircular table-top attached to it. From the mantelpiece he took a sucked lollipop, and before giving it to the child he nibbled a bit off it. The child ceased its crying and battered the lollipop against the sides of the stool. The greyhound slunk out from under the sofa and cautiously licked the sides of the stool and the chips of lollipop that had fallen on the floor.

'Get out, you brute!' said Kate, opening the scullery door and assisting the dog to the yard. 'There's enough traffic in this house without you.'

Johnny raised his head, took the nails from his mouth, and then impulsively withheld from comment. He waled into the sole vigorously, mapping it with a curve of nails; then he threw the mended boot to Frankie. 'If they don't do you, you can go in your bare feet, for there's not another nail in the house. Many's a time I went in my bare feet along country roads that'd have cut welts out on you — and a cold school into the bargain. But now you've steam pipes — palaces they are, and little good they seem to do you. You're soft, the lot of you.'

He searched the back of St. Patrick for his collar. 'Did any of you see my collar? I left it there last night and now it's gone.'

'That's no place for a collar,' Kate answered him. 'You leave everything at your heels.'

He rummaged angrily in the chest of drawers, tossing everything on to the floor. 'I can't leave a blessed thing about this house but somebody must
10

meddle with it. I suppose this is part of Mary's work — a preparation of tidiness before she leaves for the convent. I wish she would practise on somebody else.'

'Now, Johnny, you shouldn't have said that before the children. Sure she mightn't get away at all. It's somebody strong the nuns want and not a delicate thing like our Mary.'

Frankie and Peter raced into the scullery when they heard a commotion on the stairs, for they wanted to be at the tap before their sisters took command or the father spread himself out with razor, soap, and paper. The three little girls gathered round the fire, the youngest, about five, carrying a rag doll with straw sticking out of its knees. They all giggled when Frankie stumbled out of the scullery with his eyes shut and his hands clawing for a towel. Kate moved from the fire to the table, skimming the bread with the melted butter and placing two slices beside each mug. Lena, the eldest of the girls, helped to dress her two sisters, buttoning the backs of their frocks with a flourish of pride. She wiped their faces with a damp cloth and tied up their stockings that had fallen in folds over their shoes.

Seven at the table; and the child in his chair turned an enamel plate upside down and battered it with a spoon. Kate gave him a sugared crust and curved his fingers round it. There was silence now. The lark flitted about the cage and began to sing. A glittering sun glided through the window, shone on the wet sod of grass, and made shadows with the husks that floated on the white drinking vessel. It was only a blink of sun, for a coat of clouds soon covered it, and rain fell again, combing its cold way through the sooty air. A milk-cart rattled up the street, its wheels crushing the sodden newspaper and leaving shadow-tracks on the road. At the backs of the houses the rain rattled on the bin lids, formed

11

pools on the waste ground, hung files of trembling drops on the clothes-lines, and filled up the square patch where Johnny had cut his sod.

He had cut it at the top of a shelving river bank where patches of green had not yet been scuffed by the boys who played football or the children who had dug caves and covered them with rusty corrugated tin. The river this morning was the colour of clay. It was in flood, and piles of tin cans with loose lables were carried under the arch near the brick fields; it flowed down past the backs of more houses, under arches, past football grounds with tin advertisements and away under roads to the sewage of the city and the open sea. In the summer the same river would be almost dry, its big stones encrusted with clay, and here and there under the arches black sluggish pools that stank when stirred by children who came to shout and listen to their echoes sharpening from the curved walls. The river itself came from the mountain that overlooked the backs of the houses. At one time it had been contaminated by the soapy outflow from a bleach works and a steamy exudation from a cotton mill. But these were closed down now and there was nothing to discolour the river except the natural clay from the banks or the dregs that came from the empty tins that were tossed into it.

When Johnny had been cutting the sod he had gazed at the desolate mill chimneys and their ragged windows. 'This wing of the city is done,' he had said to himself, 'and when the brick yard goes there'll be nothing left.' He had heard the snoring pump sucking up water from the flooded brick fields and he felt that a time would come when all the clay would be wrested from the soil. Already two pits had been dug too deep and they were now crater-like lakes where the children sailed boats on a summer's day.

Johnny, himself, had worked in the cotton mill,

12

coming in from the country, marrying, and settling down. But since the closing of the mill he had got odd jobs about the docks and now he had taken to carrying round travellers' hampers in his handcart. He looked worried now, sitting with his family around him, some of them whimpering for another piece of bread. Upstairs was his eldest son waiting for the children to go out and for peace to decend upon the house before he'd stir. Kate was sending Frankie up to him with a mug of tea. 'Tell him to get up at once. I want him to distemper the room for your granny coming,' and she glanced over at Johnny who sat brooding, his brown eyes without a flicker of recognition.

'Do you hear me, Johnny?' she added, knocking the table with her knuckles. 'I think I'll get Hugh to give the room a lick of distemper. You've some there in the bucket. It's warmer than the cold grey that's on it. What do you say?'

She got up from the table and pushed open the room door. Handkerchiefs lay in a folded heap on the little table and near them a stump of a candle stood in its own grease. The bed was made and covered with a heavy quilt, but the room was dark because of the ivy that grew on the only window which overlooked the yard.

'Them boys have the wall destroyed with striking matches on it. When it gets the new coat of distemper let them put as much as a thumb-mark on it and I'll warm their listeners. Do you hear that, all of you?' and she turned to Frankie and Peter who were finishing their breakfast. Peter looked at her sideways, and when she had gone into the room and Johnny at her heels, he spied the purse on the shelf. The clock struck nine. The little girls got their cotton schoolbags from the back of the sofa and with their hair tied with wrinkled ribbon and old ties they made off for school. The father and mother still talked and debated in the room, and suddenly Peter rose from the table, snatched the purse from the shelf, and stole a penny.

'I'll tell!' said Frankie, frowning at him, the enamel mug in his hands.

Peter stared back at him and with tightened lips he shook a threatening fist. Lifting up his school bag he made off, Frankie shouting: 'Mother, we're away.'

A great stillness spread over the house. Johnny came out of the room. 'I'll take the handcart and if there's nothing doing to-day I'll get the lend of a bike and ride down to the old woman again. But let this be the last time!'

He shaved quickly and went out. He had no overcoat and never wore one, not even in the coldest days of winter. As he opened the rain-shining door he looked out upon the chilled waste ground with its puddles and bare clothes-lines. His handcart rested against a disused goat shed and attached to the wheel of the cart was a chain and padlock. When he had first bought the cart the boys of the street gave each other rides on it and when they had finished they sent it flying down the shelving bank of the river. Johnny found it there the next morning, its legs in the air and one spoke broken. After that he had bought a padlock and on the side of his cart on a piece of black tin he painted his name in white letters:

J. GRIFFIN
7 RIVER STREET
BELFAST

He was pushing his handcart down the waste ground when Kate came running towards him, her face pale. 'Johnny, did you take one of the pennies from the purse?'

He shook his head.

'I've searched everywhere. I wanted to get a good marrow bone for a pot of soup.'

'Ach, don't worry about it. It'll turn up.'

14

'It'll not turn up. That Peter fella has taken it. And you couldn't believe a word he'd swear. You'll have to give him a good flogging this time. God knows how he'll turn out if you let him away with it.'

'Don't you worry, I'll fix him . . . Now don't keep me back. I should have been away an hour ago.'

Brusquely he pushed off and she watched him and the rain falling on his coat and navy trousers.

'Och, God help him, he's not bad. When he was making good money in the mill he was decent with it.' She sighed as she bolted the yard door and went into the house. And when she looked at the bare table and the empty mugs a cry broke from her.

From upstairs Hugh began to whistle and then to sing. Presently he came into the kitchen, his black hair dishevelled, a butt of a cigarette in his mouth. His face was angular, and when he sucked at the butt hollows came in his cheeks.

'Get us another drop of tea — I'm foundered and famished.' He yawned loudly and shook the tea-pot that stewed at the side of the hob.

'That's for Mary; you got your share . . . Hurry up now and get the room distempered for your granny. And don't open that front door to-day without having a squeak through the curtain — it may be the rent man. When your granny comes we'll be able to face him and give him a bit of our mind for not mending the slates over the scullery; I see the rain-damp on the ceiling again.'

'Have you got the distemper and the brush? — for I'm not going to start borrowin' a morning like that.' He inhaled the last dregs of his cigarette and emitted the smoke in dribbles.

'Everything's ready, and when Mary comes in she'll give you a hand to shift the bed.'

The lark began to sing and from the street a man shouted hoarsely: 'Gather up! Any oul' rags, jam-pots, or bottles.'

Hugh with his hands in his pockets stood at the window looking at the rag-man pushing his handcart through the rain; He had a long overcoat on him that trailed the street and on the peak of his cap a curve of rain-drops. The rain mattered little to him, for he stopped and sat on one of the shafts, rummaging in an inside pocket for a cigarette.

'Gather up!' he shouted again after he had managed to light a cigarette.

Balloons — red, green, blue, and yellow — nodded on an upright stick that was lashed to the side of the cart. The rain beat on them with a hollow sound and slipped greasily down their sides. A few paper windmills, sogged and lifeless, dropped from a corner, and below them was a heap of damp rags and a shining collection of bottles. A little girl with a coat over her head ran towards the cart with a jam-pot. She selected a yellow balloon and dashed out of the rain.

'Here, Hugh, call him over and see if you can knock a few pence out of him for them bottles and them few rags.'

Hugh rapped the window, and the little man came over to the door.

'There's four good porter bottles, three jam-pots — one glass one — and a bundle of woollen rags. What do you say for the lot?'

The rag-man with forefinger and thumb sorted out the sour-smelling garments: 'I wouldn't say wool — cotton I'd say,' and he held up a tattered semmit and stretched the fabric across his finger. 'Cotton I'd say!' and with pretended disapproval threw it at his feet.

'Pure wool,' said Hugh. 'It was stamped on the back and front when it was bought,' and he looked at the blue eyes of the rag-man. He was so thin that he felt he could pull him out by the neck of the coat without unloosing a button.

The rag-man took off his cap and shook the rain

from it. 'I'll give three balloons for the lot.'

Hugh laughed. 'And what do you think I'd do with baloons? There's no kids in this house.'

'Here, I'll tell you what. I'll give you twopence — take it or leave it.'

'I'm selling rags too,' said Hugh. 'Sure I could get a halfpenny each anywhere for the bottles.'

'I'll give you twopence halfpenny. There's no money for rags nowadays.'

Hugh felt his mother nudging him.

'Have you any fags on you?' Hugh asked coaxingly. 'Give me twopence halfpenny and two fags — and the bundle's yours.'

'It's a bargain,' said the rag-man, lifting up the tail of his coat and foraging for his money and the cigarettes. He handed Hugh two gritty pennies and a wet halfpenny.

'Ye'll give us a balloon too; it'll please the child,' Kate put in, emerging from behind Hugh.

The rag-man gathered up the bundle and flung them with a rattle into his cart. He came back with a red balloon in his hand.

'Ye wouldn't have an oul' spare boot that'd fit me?' and he turned up his right boot and they could see his bare foot sticking through the sole.

'It's what we haven't got about the place,' said Kate. 'But I could give you an oul' sack to cover your windmills,' and she retrieved the bag which she had flung into the coal-hole.

The door closed. Hugh lit one of the cigarettes. 'Where's the distemper? I'm ready now for anything.'

Chapter II

Since early morning the rain had continued to fall, and at half-twelve the children slushed in hungry from school. The door of the wee room was ajar and there was the smell of cigarette smoke and the

17

splash of a brush as Hugh distempered the walls. Now and again he whistled and the rattling of the bucket handle denoted a change of position. A streaky path of blue drops trailed across the kitchen into the room.

Peter came in and recklessly tossed his schoolbag on to the sofa, and when his mother eyed him he avoided her, going upstairs and pulling things about in pretence of a search. When he came down again there were bowls of broth on the table and a potato swimming in each of them.

'Come here you, Peter!' his mother called him, catching him by the shoulder and staring into his black eyes. 'What'd you go near my purse for?'

'I never!' he lied to her.

'I can see the black lies on your tongue — the devil has his arms round you. Turn out your pockets.'

'I didn't take your penny!'

'How'd you know it was a penny was taken?'

His face reddened and he turned out his pockets. A halfpenny jingled on to the floor and rolled on its side under the sofa.

'What'd you do with the other halfpenny?'

'I saw him eating sweets at the school gate,' Lena put in.

'Mind you your own business and don't inform. Take your soup. Peter will tell all himself. Now, like a good boy, why did you take it?'

He looked down at his wet boots with their brass eye-holes, and felt the cold slime oozing through the thin soles. He didn't speak.

'All right,' his mother continued. 'To-night when your father comes home he'll put the thieving out of your head. Sit down now and take your dinner. You're lucky to get any — a good starving you need!'

His three sisters and Frankie watched him in silent awe. His black hair fell in a fringe over his brow and threads hung from the frayed cuffs of his brown jersey. His eyes stared in front of him, blank and lifeless, but his mind was alive. Before the coming of night he would run away. He would go to his granny's, and farmers passing on carts would give him a lift. It was thirty miles to his granny's — he had been there once on a lorry.

With his schoolbag under his arm he went out on to the street again and didn't wait for his brother. He ran round the back of the houses, over the cindery waste ground, down the steep river bank, and stood under the arch. The river swirled round him in a clayey flood, making his head dizzy. There was a cold suck of air under the arch and water dripped in a steady stream from the roof, and before it had time to make ripples it was carried off by the flood. Far off was the bright cave of light that marked the end of the arch. Factory horns blew intermittently, and in his mind he saw the boys in school standing in their yellow desks. The horns ceased and a great hollowness filled the air. It would be geography now and the glossy map would be unrolled and hung over the blackboard. He could see the master calling Frankie and saying: 'Where is Peter?' The master, perhaps, would disbelieve him and send a boy down to the house. Peter came out quickly from under the arch, and hid his school-bag under a clump of stones. He clambered up the wet slope of the bank, ran up a few streets, and came on to the Falls Road.

Outside the library he saw three bicycles. He stood beside the smallest of them. He looked around and with casual pretence examined the makers name which was designed on the frame. Slowly his hand slid over the silver handle-bars and in a few minutes he had it down the steps, his leg was over the saddle, and he was pedalling wildly. He never looked behind. Up the Antrim Road he raced, and twice the wheels caught in the tram-lines, nearly

19

throwing him. The rain still fell and it trickled down his hair and into his mouth. But he enjoyed it. His mind stretched forward to his granny's and already he was framing lies to tell to her. She'd be glad to see him and she'd take off his clothes, wrap him in a blanket, and let him sleep at the foot of her bed. She had done that when he had stayed three days with her and had fallen into a river while trying to stab trout with a fork.

When he reached the end of the tram-lines a gush of freedom surged through him. In front lay open country with trees shedding their leaves. The telegraph poles were glossy with rain and overhead the wires trembled as a flock of starlings settled upon them and then took off again wing-rushing through the air. Dead leaves lay in drifts along the edges of the road and their smell warmed the air. The wheels of the bicycle hissed in the rain and Peter began to sing:

'Oh, it's nice to get up in the morning,
But it's nicer to stay in bed . . .'

Ten miles from Belfast he halted at a watchman's hut. One part of the road had been dug up and he had to wait until a queue of in-going traffic had passed. With his bicycle leaning against his back he held out his hands to the watchman's brazier which sizzled in the rain and sent parching coke-fumes down his throat. He coughed, but the old watchman sitting smugly withing the hut half-shut his eyes, nodded his head in a doze, and paid no heed to him. Rain jumbled on a bundle of tea-cans hanging from one nail at the side of the hut, sheets of wire lay half-covered with soaking sand, and picks were propped against a gleaming tar barrel. Everything was desolate, and Peter wished that the watchman would take compassion on him and invite him to sit for awhile within the golden shelter of the hut. He coughed deliberately and the old man opened his sleepy eyes, stretched out a long cleck and without rising to his feet pulled the three-legged brazier closer to the hut. Peter got ready to move off and then he noticed for the second time the bundle of tea-cans hanging from one nail. Slyly he approached them, raised his hand, and with one swipe sent them clattering off the nail on to the road. There was a stumble in the hut; Peter's leg was over the saddle and behind him the old man cursed and pegged stones.

At Antrim town he noticed by a church clock that it was ten minutes past three. He free-wheeled down the hill, but soon had to jam on the brakes for a drove of cattle blocked his way. He hopped off and inquired the way to Toome.

'Ten miles!' the drover answered him, 'and a bloody big hill that'll raise blisters on ye. How far have ye come?'

Peter hesitated, remembering that he had stolen the bicycle: 'I came from Downpatrick.'

'Ye did — like hell!'

'My father died this morning and I was sent to tell my granny that lives at Toome.'

The drover eyed him quizzically: 'Ye better be goin' on your way.' And as Peter rode off the drover shouted after him: 'Walk up the hill I told you about or ye'll bust yer braces.'

Three miles beyond Antrim he stopped at a small farm-house and begged for bread. A young woman brought him in and gave him a seat at the turf fire. She wore a pair of man's boots laced with cord, and near the fire a baby lay asleep in a cradle. Peter sat on a stool inside the glowing curve of heat while steam arose from his clothes and water trickled from his boots.

As she spread a newspaper on the table the young woman regarded him with great sympathy and plied him with questions. He told her how his father had died and how he had been sent to bring the news to his granny.

21

'My poor child, you'll be famished and foundered afore you reach Toome. It'll soon be dark, for the daylight's scarce these evenings . . . And yiv eatin' nothin' since twelve o'clock. Ah, my poor, poor son! And yiv no brothers nor sisters! God take care of you.'

Her voice was so mournful and wrung with pity that Peter winked tears into his eyes to please her.

Through the open door he saw the rain fall like fine wire and drops hanging on the ragged hedges. A robin chirped and when it lit on a twig drops fell to the ground. Wet-drenched hens came in at the door and the young woman swished at them with a cloth: 'Shoosh on out o' that ye'd think ye never saw mate.'

On the fire blobs of soot fell into a pot of yellow meal and Peter drew the woman's attention towards it.

'That's a sign of bad weather,' she said. 'There'll be more rain and maybe a storm.'

She put on the kettle, and with twigs and withered potato tops fed the fire. Then she searched in the room and found an old coat of her husband's.

'Put that on you; it'll turn a shower.'

He stood up. The sleeve fell loosely over his hands. He was like a scarecrow, and she smiled as she folded them back and pinned them to the proper length: 'It'll do you till you get to Toome.' And after taking a good bowl of tea he was ready for the road.

When he went outside each step he took sent a spurt of pain through his legs and he laughed nervously. He pedalled almost without force. The bicycle seemed heavier and once or twice he got off and examined it to see if anything were catching in the mud-guards. The rain was slackening and the solid mass of sky was breaking into loose lumps of cloud. Leaves whirled through the air and crickled in the thorny hedges.

He walked up the mile-long hill at Randalstown and at the top he saw across the naked fields the water-gleam of Lough Neagh. A young moon like a flake of cloud leaned its shoulder on top of a far-off mountain. Peter realized it would soon be dark. Down a hill he raced and the breeze chilled him under the arm-pits and the heavy coat bellied over the saddle. At Toome the quiet lamps of the little homes were being lit and doors were shut against the night air. And then he came to his granny's.

Quietly he got off the bicycle. The hens had gone to roost and only a cat lay on the window-sill, and into buckets at the side of the door water dripped from the thatch. At the bare window he saw her sitting in the fire-glow, her silver spectacles glinting, and her finger following the words in her prayer-book. Her lips moved and now and again she turned her right hand as if rolling a ball of wool. She licked her thumb to turn a page in her prayer-book and then she saw him at the window. She opened the door and he stood in front of her, outlined against the light from the sky. She took off her spectacles and slewed him round so that the light from the sky shone in his face: 'Sweet God in Heaven, is it Peter?'

He didn't speak. His face was streaked with rain and his eyes big with fear and exhaustion.

She gripped his shoulders and his arms: 'You're soaking! Come in! Come on in till I gather my senses and get my breath.' She put her spectacles in her prayer-book and put them inside a trunk from which there gushed a thick smell of camphor. She piled on turf, hooked a blind to the window that looked out on the road, and in the embrasure of the back window she lit a candle. All the time Peter never stirred.

'Get your clothes off at once before you get your death,' and she smiled when she saw him take off the man's coat with cuffs pinned back.

'What's wrong, Peter? Where on earth did you come from?' and she looked at him dubiously. His mind went numb and he burst into tears.

'Don't cry, Peter, my son,' and she placed his head on her lap. 'Sure I know; and you'll get a nice mug of tea and a good sleep and you'll tell me in the morning.'

She began to undress him, throwing the wet slop of clothes on the floor: 'Poor child, your arm's as thin as a ruler! Here's a cloth to cover your shame.' She got a bucket and washed his legs, rubbed life into him with a towel, and later wrapped him in a blanket and he sat at the fire like a helpless old man, a newspaper under his feet. On a table beside the candle-lit window she placed the bucket of clothes, and he saw the reflection of her face in the pane, the dark bulges below her eyes, the creases coming and going on her sleeves as she dipped and wrung out the clothes. It was very quiet now; the kettle was simmering and the candle spat when specks of water skited over it.

From a corner of the dresser she took a black bottle and ladled two spoonfuls of poteen into his tea.

'What's in that, Granny?' he asked.

'It's something the fairies make in Lough Beg,' and she took a spoonful herself and licked the cork.

And as he sipped the tea and it scorched with a little poteen his tongue loosened and he talked to please her: 'I dreamt last night about you. I dreamt you were sick.'

'God forbid, child dear. Take your tea and eat up them heels of a loaf; they'll be good for your grinders. I hadn't time to bake a griddle of bread and that oul' shopbread fills my stomach full of wind — I don't know how you all thrive on it.'

'But you weren't sick like a woman in a hospital,' he continued, as if she hadn't spoken at all. 'You

24

were sick because every time you looked out of the door you saw a hen coming with a flock of chickens from the demesne. And there were so many hens and so many chickens ye began to cry because you wondered how you could feed them all. And the chickens began to cheep all night with hunger and you got no sleep. Then you took bad and I saw you in bed sick and hens roosting on the bed-rail. And I thought the dream was true and I told nobody and I said I'd go down myself to see you.'

'And you dreamt that. There's no sense in dreams. But when you dream about the dead pray hard for their souls.'

'And I dreamt other things, Granny!'
She looked up from her stool and saw his two hands encircling the mug and his two eyes sunk in his head: 'Yer dying with sleep. I think I'll put you to bed.'

Then she began to ask about all in the house — and the baby: 'I can't remember his name . . . Oliver! It's a funny name that! — it reminds me of an egg.'

Presently she brought him up to the room and put him at the foot of the bed. The quiet light from the candle came through the open door. He lay awake for awhile and heard her moving about the kitchen. Her shadow, big and bulky, filled the door or stretching up the wall mingled with the cold gloom under the thatch. She would give out a cough, a complaint, and he would hear her beads rattling as she said her prayers for the night. The bed smelt of dust. A rising wind swooped against the window and he could feel it brushing over the thatch. Its sound made everything bleak and lonely and filled the night with dread. He put out his finger and touched the damp, flaky limewash on the walls; then he lay back and saw in the light from the kitchen the broken cobwebs on the rafters hanging down like dirty cord.

The front door was opened and a draught blew around his head.

'Puss, puss, where are you, you thief? Go on out and enjoy yourself — that night will freeze a few of your fleas.' He could hear the dark flurry of the wind in the hedges, and he pressed deeper into the bed. The door was closed and bolted. Her shadow circled round the room again and he heard her spit on the hearth and scrape the ashes. She came into the room and went out again. Then at last she blew out the candle and the bed whimpered as she climed into it.

'Lie well over for I'm sure you kick like a mule . . . Ah, thank God for bed,' and she blew out her breath loudly.

He lay close to the wall. 'Are ye asleep, Peter?' and she stretched out her stockinged feet and touched him. He didn't answer though he winked to himself in the dark. There was a great plunge of heat from the hot jar which she had wrapped in a flannel and placed at the foot of the bed.

She began to twist and turn and he held grimly to a corner of the blankets.

'Have ye plenty of clothes?' she asked. There was no reply. 'Ach, the creature, he's done to the world after that journey. He'll be as stiff as a plank in the morning!' After that, listening to the rumble of the wind, he slept.

Back at home they did not miss him until tea-time. Then the questions and cross-examination began: his little sisters telling that he had mitched and Frankie getting red to the ears. Then they heard the dog barking at the back door and the rattle of the handcart crunching over the cinders of the waste ground. In a few minutes Johnny came in, but Kate had already ceased questioning about Peter. The gas was lit. Johnny was in good form, and as he came in he noticed a few distemper spots on the red tiles and sniffed the air.

'So Hugh has been busy again,' and he opened the room door and saw Mary hemming handkerchiefs by candlelight. He peered at the blue walls: 'I don't know, but that room seems colder after its wash — it's like a morgue.'

Kate shrugged her shoulders: 'Wait'll you get a drop of tea in you and Hugh hangs up the pictures and ye'll find it much warmer.'

Hugh was sitting at the fire with a Wild West magazine in his hands. Frankie sat on the fender learning Butler's *Penny Catechism*: 'Sixth not to solemnize marriage at forbidden times nor to marry persons within the forbidden degrees of kindred or otherwise prohibited by the church nor clandestinely.'

'Here,' said Hugh. 'Are you going to entertain us to that the night again. I'm tired listening to you. Give it a rest.'

The little girls, Lena and Ann and Rita, sat on the stairs playing school, shouting and counter-shouting and hammering the wall with a stick.

Kate fussed over them like a brooding hen: 'Here the lot of you — yiv got your teas; it's time you were all in bed. My head's astray with you in the house all day. Please God, the sun will shine to-morrow.'

Johnny took off his damp coat and hung it on the back of a chair. Frankie still hummed at his catechism.

'Well, how did you get on the day? Any luck?' Kate asked as she filled the tea-pot.

'I done well, but it'll be the last for a long time. When I went down to the back of the hotel there was three there in front of me with empty handcarts and the rain peltin' heavens hard. I put my handcart at the end of the line and waited my turn. Then the porter put out his head and whistled to me. I went up to him. "I've a good traveller," says he, "but you'll have to give me a half-a-dollar commission before I'll engage you." I looked at his hungry-looking face for a minute and was ready to tell him to go to blazes, but then I thought I'd better accept his terms. I carried out the hampers and he told me to go round to the front of the hotel and he'd introduce me to my man. When I was pushing off, the other barrow-men glared at me: "Why did you take the so-and-so's stingy terms," they said. "What hell right has he to ask for commission? Who's doin' the job." But anyway, I came round to the front of the hotel and there was my traveller: a nice young man, no bigger than Peter — Scotch he was, but a real toff. He took out his wee note-book: "Bring the samples round to Hyams in North Street and I'll see you there in ten minutes."

'Round I went and I held his umbrella over the hampers till he lifted out some samples. He had a good morning, and at lunch-hour he gave me two bob to get a feed. I went to one of them atin' houses at Smithfield and ordered a good tightener of soup and stew. And I sat near the window keeping my eye cocked on the hampers and the handcart — there's a lot of smart fellas about the same Smith-field! The evening was better still. "You seem to have brought me a bit of luck," says my friend when he handed me fifteen shillings for the day. "I'll be back to your city again and I'll drop you a card," says he, and he wrote my address in his note-book. I touched my cap and pushed the hampers round to the back of the hotel and rang the bell in the wall.

'In a few minutes out comes my yellow-faced porter rubbing his hands and smiling like a hangman. "You had a good day?" says he. I never answered him and I carried in the hampers. "You had a good day and a good man?" says he again. "Mr. Fraser always pays up well."

'I looked at him straight between his ferrety eyes, his hair well oiled and smelling like a chemist's shop. And then I thought about the rain and the day I put in, splashed to the neck with gutters and my feet in a slobber the whole day. The handcart was cleared and he stretched out his paw: "Four shillings I want or you'll get no more jobs from me!" says he. "Four shillings," says I, "I thought you agreed to half a dollar."

' "No, I never," says he. "I wouldn't give Mr. Fraser for less."

' "You agreed to two and sixpence, and I think it's too damned much!" says I.

' "Do you!" says he, sticking his thin face close to mine.

' "Fork out three and six and we'll part as friends."

"All right," says I. I put my hand in my pocket and then something came over me. I looked at his hungry paw and before I knew what had happened I raised my fist and with one clout sent him sprawling over the hampers: "Go to hell now," says I, "and work for your three and sixpence." '

Hugh had put down his Wild West magazine and was listening proudly: 'You did right! I hope you flattened him with a good dinger.'

Kate stood at the fire with folded arms and sucked in her lips when Johnny had finished. She said nothing, but in her own mind she knew that he was barred for ever from that hotel.

Johnny had his legs crossed, his thumbs in the armholes of his waistcoat. He stood up and counted out fifteen shillings: 'The stew and broth came to ninepence. Give us a bit of a fry, Kate, for I'm sure the pan's red with rust.'

She saw him take off his collar and hang it over St. Patrick. He was preparing himself for a night's rest. When the tea was over she'd tell about Peter. She called Mary out of the room to go to the shop.

After Johnny had regaled himself with bacon and eggs he sat on the sofa: 'I'm as weary as an old horse and I've a big brute of a corn that has tortured the life out of me the whole day — a corn's a quare heart-scald.' No one spoke and no one was enthusiastic about his complaints — all were thinking of Peter.

Twice the mother halted in her clearing away of the dishes, and with one hand on her hinch and the other resting on the table she sought for easy words to say to him, but for some reason she remained silent. And then as he bent down to untie his laces she abruptly and awkwardly spoke: 'Peter hasn't been in all day and he mitched from school and stole a penny.'

Johnny raised his head, the exhausted look gone from his eyes: 'Well, that's a scoundrel for you. That's a nice cup of tea after a hard day's work. Up to his tricks again! Well, when I lay my hands on him he'll never mitch nor steal in his life again. There's a bad drop in that Peter fella; and I don't know under God who he take after . . . Frankie, do you know where he is?'

'No, Father. I went on to school by myself after my dinner and I don't know where he went.'

His father frowned at him, and Frankie with innocent eyes looked down at his catechism.

'I suppose we'll have to look for him. Come on, Hugh, and we'll search the brickyard kilns.'

They went out by the back and across the dark waste ground. A scrap of a moon gave little light, but here and there the star-shine skimmed the puddles. The mouldy smell of the river oozed up to them and they could hear the rush and jabble of the water as it sped under the arch. Their feet sank in the cart-ruts as they crossed the bridge to the brick yard. The tall chimney dribbled smoke and through the air came the throb of an engine and the water-suck of the pump. There was great heat from the kilns and a few stray donkeys moved out when Johnny and Hugh approached. They stumbled over tramps who were lying with their backs to the warm kilns, and Hugh struck matches and inquired if any of them had seen a young lad in a brown jersey. None of them had seen him. They passed the watchman going on his rounds, his flash-lamp throwing a bull's-eye of light on the ground. He hadn't seen him either and they went away disconsolately and on their way back searched the goat's shed. Hugh's wet slippers were red with brick dust.

'There's no sign of him anywhere,' said Johnny as he came in. 'That night would skin you,' and he rubbed his red hands and held them to the bars of the grate.

Mary was crying. Kate gazed at them anxiously: 'A policeman called when you were out. Peter was seen stealing a bicycle from the Falls Road library.'

'We're all disgraced now,' Mary added tremulously. 'It'll be in the paper and I'll never get to the convent. I don't know what's come over this house — there's no luck nor grace in it.'

Kate gave a forced smile: 'Don't take it so ill, Mary. Sure he's only a bit of a lad with no sense and people will understand. There'll be no proceedings if the bike's returned safe and sound.'

'When I get him I'll break his back,' Johnny assured them, hanging up his cap behind the kitchen door. 'Whatever bad company that fella has got into of late.'

'He hangs around with Hugo Neeson,' added Frankie excitedly.

'Who asked you for an opinion? You should be in bed hours ago. Go on up now.'

Quietly Frankie put away his book and ascended the stairs; Kate looked after him and smiled reassuringly.

They all sat near the fire speculating on Peter's whereabouts and wondering what had he done with the bicycle.

'I bet anything he's in Toome!' Hugh suggested.

31

'He'd never make it in that rain,' said Johnny.

Mary's hands opened and closed, her teeth bit into her lower lip. 'Maybe he'd do away with himself.'

'Nonsense, child! What put a thought like that into your head? Go on to bed, Mary, and don't worry about him any more. Here's a bit of paper to light your candle. He'll be all right and he'll turn up as happy as larry. I bet you he's snug now in his granny's bed and the bicycle will be in the byre out of harm's way.'

'If to-morrow's a good day I'll hit the road for Toome,' said Johnny.

'And you'll have Peter and granny back with you,' Kate brightened.

Johnny tugged at his boot-laces and one of them broke: 'If it's raining I'll not go at all and I'll put the police on that young blackguard's track. He's the makings of a promising boy.'

Chapter III

It was midday. Peter had just finished his breakfast and his granny had sent him on the bicycle to buy a few cuts of red wool, and before going she had put a piece of the required pattern in an envelope and pinned it inside his jersey: 'Tell them it's for Maggie Griffin of Killyfast and they'll make no mistake.'

She stood at the door and watched him mount stiffly on his bicycle. The thin sunlight shone on her sallow face and a cat ran up her apron and sat on her shoulder. White hens pecked around her feet. The air was cold and she had a light grey shawl about her shoulders and a red flannel on her head. She shaded her eyes and gazed across the damp road. Two leaves flitted through the air and enmeshed themselves on wire-netting that covered a gap in the hedge. She was about to turn into the house when Johnny Griffin came riding up to the very door.

'First Peter and now Johnny — it's like an excursion. I'm glad to see you. You've got thinner since I saw you last. And I wish to God ye'd leave your moustache alone — you've clipped it away to a stump.'

Awkwardly he kissed her on the side of the cheek and went in. The fire was low and potatoes were boiling. He gathered up the stray coals with the tongs and put on turf.

'The city and its ways hasn't put the handling of tongs out of you. I must get something for the hens. Would you get me a go-of-water from the well?'

'And ye tell me that wee blackguard is here. When did he arrive?'

Her old mind floundered for words to answer him. His lips were tight and he held his cap over his right hand and kept turning it as he spoke. She manoeuvred for time:

'Why, Johnny, do you always get your hair clipped so close? Ye'd think you were just out of jail. And them head scars make you look like a hen in the moult.'

'Things is still bad with us and it suits my pocket to get a decent hair-cut when I'm at it. Where's this Peter fella?'

'D'ye know, if you had that black moustache off, yer the dead spit of Robert Emmet. G'on down to the room and have a look at his picture. He's as fresh-looking as the day ye made the cork-frame with all the old porter bottle corks. D'ye mind that?'

He nodded indifferently and launched into a minute account of Peter: how he had mitched from school, stole a penny from his mother that could ill afford it, pinched a bicycle from the Falls Road library, and how they had searched for him all night and how the police were scouring the whole

33

countryside.

'Oh, the rascal, and he told me a boy lent him the bike.'

'He's a disgrace to our name.'

Sunlight fell through the open door and a hen came in, snatched a crust from the floor and raced out again.

'Och, Johnny, make allowances for the young. Ye weren't a model of the virtues when you were young. Sure you raided orchards galore and mitched the next day. You must be easy on him and he'll never do it again. I'll get him to promise on his two bended knees when he comes back from the village.'

'He has promised me time and again he'd mend his ways. The police will deal with him this time.'

The flames twirled round the sods of turf. The old woman patted her knee, but didn't speak. Johnny lifted the bucket from the corner of the dresser and went out.

He opened the wooden gate at the side of the house and crossed the field that sloped to the well. He noticed the tracks of her feet and her stick. 'She shouldn't come down here alone,' he said to himself, bending down over the black pool and brushing the floating leaves away with the bucket. He took a drink of the ice-cold water. The well was shadowed with quiet and a thin wind crisped through the overhanging hedges. He saw places where he used to do jumps as a boy, bushes where he had found nests, and above his head two poplar trees, cold as frost. He remembered making hay on warm days, lying on his back, and looking up at the poplar leaves flashing like many wings, and how his father had said: 'Johnny, Johnny, no wind can sneak by a poplar tree,' and both had leaned back and listened to the rainy sound of their leaves.

He put down the bucket and crushed his way through the hedge into the neighbouring field. It sponged under his feet; it required stubbing; and he recalled how, when his father had worked it, it had yielded crops of corn and potatoes. But all that land had been mortgaged and nothing remained now only the house and the small field with the well. The shape of the land had changed but little in the course of thirty years. Here and there a blown-down tree was honeycombed with holes, hedges had grown taller and wider at the legs, but the fields had not changed.

In his walk he had come to the top of a hill where he saw far away the River Bann scything through flat soggy country spreading itself out in Lough Beg where he saw the tree-covered island and the spire of a ruined church. He sighed and breathed in the fresh-cold air: 'It's no wonder the oul' wan wants to stay in it. It's a good country for them that can make a living in it.' Below him was the demesne, its walls tumbling, and rabbits running wild in its naked fields. Many's a wintry night he had poached for them when the air was coarse with frost, the hailstones clustered in the hoof-marks and the rabbits big as sheep against the moon.

He turned back to the well and where the bucket had laid there was a sharp circle in the mud and the marks of his mother's stick.

'Impatient as ever,' he said to himself as he walked up the field towards the white house.

'You're a nice one to send for a bucket of water. I thought you'd gone to the lough for it and the poor hens eating the lime-wash off the walls.'

He didn't answer, but sat down at the hearth, placing a few briars on the fire.

'Watch and don't jag yourself with the crabbed tops of them briars . . . The spuds will be boiled in a minute.'

She noticed the melancholy look in his eyes: 'Well, Johnny, what ails you?'

He stroked the ashes with the tongs and scraped the flakes of soot off the neck of the chimney: 'I'm thinking it's not safe for an oul' woman like you to be living here your lone and going down to that slippery shough of a well and maybe fall in. And what'd happen if you took a weak turn during the night and nobody here to go for the priest. I'm worried about it.'

'Sure, Johnny, son, I can do nothing. I'm not as supple on my feet as I used to be, but my sight's good and I have neither pain nor ache.'

The cat jumped on to her lap and began to purr. She stroked it and it arched its tail and rubbed its head against her breast.

'It makes me uneasy to think of you here and a good home for you in Belfast with plenty of company.'

'Och, Johnny, I'm too old now to be changing my ways. I'm my own boss here and I can go down to the chapel of a morning or evening and say my prayers and visit the graves. I'll stay here, Johnny, and if I take sick I can get a girl to redd up the dishes and feed the hens.'

'You'll have a lovely room all to yourself and there's ivy round the window and you can come and go as you please.'

'God forgive me, but I don't like ivy round a house — I think it's unlucky,' and she stuck a fork in the potatoes and Johnny got up and teemed them for her.

'Ye needn't worry about the ivy; we could cut that down.' But she wasn't listening to him as she spread three plates on the table. She put eggs in a tin and Johnny snuggled it close to the side of the fire where it hissed and spluttered.

A bicycle bell rang and Peter came riding through the door, the cuts of red wool entwined about his neck.

'Back again, Granny!' he shouted. And I got you

a happorth of snuff with the penny you gave me and . . .' He stopped abruptly when he saw his father's ironic smile.

'Where'd you get the bicycle?' his father inquired, without taking his eyes from him.

'I got the lend of it . . .'

'You're a wee liar,' and he rose from the chair and made a swipe at him. The cat ran out through the door. 'Why don't you tell the truth!' and he gave him a clout that sent him stumbling across the floor. His granny caught him and he clung tightly to her.

'I'll never do it again,' he cried as Johnny tried to pull him from her.

'I'll not have anything like that in this house. And if that's what you'd treat me to in Belfast I'll stay where I am,' and she rubbed the back of Peter's head, at the same time noticing that the elbows were nearly out of his jersey.

'Johnny, the eggs! They'll be as hard as a stone.'

In his anger he gripped the hot handle of the tin and pulled it to the side. He sucked his thumb: 'The devil take that fella — he's unlucky. I'm after giving myself a right burn over the head of him.'

'Don't say another word to him, Johnny. He'll be a good boy. Won't you, Peter?'

'Ai, Granny,' he sniffed and rubbed the tears from his eyes with the back of his hand.

The three of them sat down to the table. Through the little window Johnny saw again the fields and the poplars with their remaining leaves fluttering in the wind.

The old woman smiled when she saw the cone-shaped paper of snuff on the table: 'There's great kindliness in the creature,' she thought to herself. 'And sure he'll grow out of his wee ways!' and she broke bread and passed the crusts to him.

'Eat plenty of spuds, son, for you've a long ride afore you.'

'And a sorry ride too,' put in Johnny, 'for the police will be waiting for him at the end of the journey.'

'Promise me, Johnny, you'll not say a word to him and maybe I'll take a run up to see that room of yours.'

'Oh, oh,' says Johnny, tilting back on the chair. 'You may bet your boots I'll not lay a hand on him, but I'm afraid nothing will save him from the police.'

Granny jammed pieces for him and darned his jersey. She made Johnny try on the coat that the young woman had given to Peter: 'It's your fit and if you leave me your own I'll mend it and send it up to you.'

In the early afternoon father and son jumped on their bicycles and made for home, the father ordering Peter to keep in front and walk up the hills. At Templepatrick they had a rest and Peter munched his bread while his father smoked.

It was dusk when they arrived at the outskirts of the city and it was dark when Johnny brought Peter to the barracks where in a bare, gas-lighted room, a large fire blazing in the grate, they sat at a long wooden table while a policeman gravely wrote down a statement from Johnny. The voice of the policeman echoing in the big room, the sight of the book and the important scratch of the pen, made Peter recoil with fear, and he kept his head lowered and peered out from under his long lashes. A policeman would come in, hang up his holster and cap, and open one of the big black boxes ranged along the wall. Every minute Peter waited for one of them to produce handcuffs and lead him off to jail.

And then his father was nudging him, and the policeman who had scribbled in the book regarded him with a studious smile: 'And is this the culprit? A dark horse in many ways!'

Peter flicked his lashes and then the tears came. 'Come on,' said his father gruffly. 'Six years you'll get on bread and water.'

Chapter IV

'There's too many petty thefts in this locality of late and the law is compelled to set an example to the other blackguards. I'm afraid Mrs. Griffin, your boy, Peter, will have to accompany me now. To-morrow he will be sent to the Industrial School . . .'

Kate wiped a chair with her apron for the policeman. Frankie who was doing his exercise at the table turned pale and Peter who had been bulking marbles on the floor had gone in under the sofa to find one which had rolled away. He was now crawling out backwards, the thread on his patched trousers breaking under the strain.

The policeman sat down, slackened his belt a couple of holes, tore a sheet from Frankie's jotter to light his pipe, and crossed his legs with satisfaction.

'Now, Missus, like a good woman be sensible and don't cry.'

'But, sir, the bicycle was returned!'

'My good woman, I am sorry to say that there are other charges against your son, Peter. On more than one occasion he has tried to pass bad money on a purblind shopkeeper across the way.' The policeman puffed at his pipe with assured importance. 'And he has stolen buns from a baker's cart and fruit from a fruit shop. We have had him under suspicion for a considerable time, I may inform you.'

Peter's black eyes opened wide and he looked up meekly at the huge policeman, and tears slid out of his eyes when he saw his mother crying. She shook her head reproachfully at him, and so tightly did he squeeze the marbles that white marks appeared on his knuckles.

'Listen here, my good woman,' the policeman continued, 'if your son, Peter, conducts himself in a proper manner and according to the rules and regulations of the Home, he'll be back to you within a year or so. It will be like a holiday for him.'

'But, sir, he'll be disgraced for all the days of his life and it will break his health.'

The policeman pushed his glazed peaked cap to the back of his head, re-crossed his legs, and spat skilfully between the bars of the grate. The chair creaked as he turned to emphasize each word with the shank of his pipe.

'Now, Missus, I am totally ashamed at an intelligent woman like you uttering such a remark. The Home will make a man of him. It isn't as if he were going to jail. He will have fields to play in. He will learn boot-making and tailoring and how to play the flute. They have a most beautiful brass band, for I have heard it myself on myriad occasions. Get him ready now, like a good woman, and we'll proceed.'

Kate slowly ascended the stairs and Peter followed her. The policeman stretched out a hand and lifted Frankie's arithmetic from the table. He frowned at the weak light from the damaged gas-mantle. Then he licked his thumb and turned the sticky pages of the arithmetic, critically rising his eyebrows or giving a surprised whistle through his teeth.

'Yes, not very far advanced, I should say. When I was your age I was capable of solving the most difficult problems in both Simple and Compound Interest, Stocks and Shares, and recurring decimals. You have the easy times at school now compared with the old days.' He opened his tunic at the neck, and placed his cap with the pipe inside it on the table. He handed the book back to Frankie, joined and unjoined his hands.

Upstairs a boot fell on the floor. Frankie fidgeted and gazed with awe at the silver numbers glinting on the policeman's collar and at the great rolls of flesh bulging on his neck.

'To test your intelligence, young man,' and he spoke so suddenly that Frankie jumped. 'How would you answer this? — Which would you rather have: a ton of half-sovereigns or a half-ton of sovereigns? . . . Think before you answer — everything comes to the man who knows how to think.'

Frankie swallowed audibly: 'They're both the same!'

'Wrong!' said the policeman, leaning back on the creaking chair and sticking his thumbs into his belt. 'Wrong, young man; those, who do not think, answer in the same perfunctory manner. Like a good boy, to-morrow give that problem to your teacher and I can assure you it will puzzle him.'

He laughed heartily, stretched out his hands for the pipe, and tapped his pockets for his matches. Frankie handed him a piece of paper and the policeman twisted it, bent forward in the chair, and stuffed it between the bars of the grate. As he lit the pipe he half-shut his eyes and Frankie wondered was he thinking out more puzzling questions. He sighed with relief when he heard his mother on the stairs, but when he saw the tears in Peter's eyes he became depressed, yawned involuntarily and bit his lip to keep from crying. Peter held his head down; the tracks of a wet comb were shining in his black hair. In his hand he carried a brown paper parcel containing a clean shirt and stockings. He was crying as he gave a sideways glance at Frankie.

'Come now! Tempus fugit!' and the policeman tightened his belt and pulled down his tunic.

Peter turned pleadingly to his mother: 'Don't let me go! I'll be good! I'll never do it again!'

'The law's the law; it can't be altered one iota. My good lady, you'll have him back in a year or two — a strong healthy boy, fit to pull a plough. And you can visit him regularly at the Home — a fine beautiful building standing in its own grounds.'

Johnny came in by the back and the policeman shook hands with him and launched into an account of the stolen bicycle, and pilfering of sweets, and the grand time he would have in the Home. Peter cried again and Johnny waved a hand and laughed brusquely: 'Crying! I wish I was going. Man dear, you'll have the time of your life — mending boots, making furniture, and playing football.'

Peter laughed nervously and his father squeezed a penny into his hand: 'Be a good boy, now, and say yer prayers morning and night.'

Johnny went out with them while Kate and Frankie stood at the door and watched them disappear down the dark street. A street lamp at each side reflected on the wet pavement. Lights were in nearly all the windows and somewhere a gramophone was playing. She was grateful for the darkness. The neighbours wouldn't see Peter going away and later on she could tell them that he had gone to the country for the good of his health. She came in and sat on the sofa and told Frankie to get on with his lessons and always to keep away from bad companions. She heard his pen scratching over the paper and she got up and busied herself about the dark scullery.

Mary came in and hung up her coat and hat in the wee room. Her dark eyes were shining, and as she lilted a song she did not notice the gloom in the house or the silence of her mother working away by herself in the scullery. She screwed up her mouth and grimaced playfully at Frankie. She bent over his book: 'You can work neater than Peter. He's slovenly and careless.' A cup rattled on a hook and she called to her mother: 'Sit down, mother, and I'll finish them.'

'Rest yourself,' she answered back in a subdued tone. 'There's only one or two left.'

Mary went to the room again and brought out a white altar cloth which she was embroidering for

42

the Foreign Missions. She spread it on her knees and meticulously drew the red-threaded needle along the Celtic design already traced on the cloth. Occasionally she would hold it out from her to examine it or she would sit with her hands idle, her mind full of the Mission class she had just left.

With other girls she had arrived early at the school-room, had lit the gas, pulled out the trestle table from the wall, dusted it and had everything prepared before Sister Dominic came panting up the stairs to them.

'So everything's in readiness, girls . . . It's rather cold in here and I think I'll light the stove,' and the nun bent down, turned on the gas, and stood back and flung the lighted matches at it. She used six matches before it finally lit with a loud bang.

'And, Mary Griffin, what have you been doing with yourself? — You've got pale,' and she pinched her cheek. 'Mind now, health before wealth. Don't work too hard!'

The hampers were dragged out and the nun commented jovially on each remnant of coloured cloth as she lifted them and bundled them on the table.

'Would a piccaninny like this?' and the nun wrapped a piece of yellow silk around her neck, joined her hands, and rolled her eyes in mock angelic fervour. Or lifting a piece of red cloth: 'Now that wouldn't make a frock for a little negro girl. Maybe, Mary Griffin, you could make a pair of boy's pants out of it — trap doors and all!' The girls giggled and bowed their heads with pretended disgust. One of them sighed and the nun raised her eyebrows: 'Now, Alice, he'll wait for you!' And Alice shrugged her shoulders: 'Oh, Sister, you're awful.'

'Now, now, if I were a young man,' the nun tapped the table with her thimble, 'I'd know good looks when I saw them.'

Then silence, the stitch stitch of the needles, and the rattle of the nun's girdle of beads as she stretched

43

across the table. The evening had all blended into a solid warmth of colour and sound: the dusty globes of gas, the shining nail-heads on the trestle table, a pitted thimble lying on its side, and the fizzle of the jam-pot of water in front of the stove. Quiet and peace! A mouse rustled in the old fireplace and all the girls had held their needles and listened.

'A mouse!' said the nun, and she rattled her feet to scare it.

Then stitch again and silence. Far away down long corridors a burst of singing from the nuns' chapel and outside the hum of the trams. Scissors snip and there's a warm smell from the clothes as they are turned. The paper rustles again and the nun rattles her feet:

'Now, girls, I think you've done heaps of work for to-night ... And, maybe, Mary Griffin will turn out the gas for me' — and Mary knew that the nun was afraid of the mouse and the groping out of the room in the darkness.

Thinking of it she sighed and her wooden embroidery hoop rolled on to the floor and under the sofa. Frankie got up from the table and fetched it for her. With her hands on her lap Kate was looking at her thoughtfully and then as if she had spoken her thoughts Mary turned to her and said: 'Where's Peter?'

Kate pretended not to hear her and she lifted the altar cloth and followed the design with her finger: 'That'll be beautiful, Mary, when you've it finished.'

Johnny came in: 'Well, that policeman was the greatest oul' cod from here to Jericho. All the way to the barrack he lectured me on the names of stars and the phases of the moon. "Why do stars twinkle?" says he. And poor wee Peter looked up at him and said, "I learnt that poem in school long ago:

Twinkle, twinkle little star
How I wonder what you are ...'

The both of us laughed at that and by the holy

44

didn't that set the peeler off his rocker and he recited lashin's of poems of all lengths and sizes . . . A decent homely peeler, but a damned oul' fool!'

Mary had put down her sewing and was looking puzzledly at her father.

Johnny went on: 'Peter nearly broke down when I was leaving him and I had to promise we'd go up to see him on Sunday.'

'Mary doesn't know about it,' interrupted Kate, and she turned to her and told about the policeman's visit to the house and how they could tell the neighbours that Peter was away to the country for the good of his health.

Mary's hands went limp and all eagerness for work drained away from them. There was always something now to break the solace of an evening, something to ravage her mind and fill her with dissatisfaction.

'Will we ever have peace?' she said despairingly. 'We try to be decent, but there's always something, something that tries to break us and keep us down.' Wearily she folded up her altar cloth and went into her room. She sat in the dark on the side of the bed. She would have to face things she told herself. What was the use of all her praying or her desire to enter a convent if she were always ready to fly from trouble. She stood up. The door was closed and below it was a crack of light from the kitchen. The window was dark except for the top pane where she saw a few stars, the ivy leaves fluttering and their tips scratching the glass. The moon broke through a gap in the clouds and a blurred shadow stretched from the crucifix on the table.

'I knew that was coming to him,' she heard her father say, after he had washed himself. 'A year in that institution will cool his heels. Don't you worry yourself about him, Kate, the same fella needed a good trouncing . . . Frankie, you better go to bed.'

'But I'm thinking of the children,' her mother's

voice was toneless. 'Poor Mary takes these things so bad. Do you think it'll bar her when she wants to enter the convent?'

'Sure it wasn't Mary stole the bicycle and she can't keep her brother under lock and key. That's not what's worrying me. I didn't do a hand's turn to-day. The handcart business is done; ye'd have thought they were going to a football match the way they were lined up at the back of the hotels the day. And them porters are a hungry crowd of hounds — they give all to their own friends,' and he sat down on the sofa, joining and unjoining the tips of his fingers, a babit of his when he was worried.

The gaslight faded, and Kate took a penny from her apron pocket and dropped it in the meter. The light strengthened. Johnny stretched himself out on the sofa, his two hands under his head. His eyes strayed from the red distempered walls to the bird sleeping in its cage and to the torn grocery calendar above his head.

'The rent man got in to-day and threatened to take proceedings at the end of the week.'

'Don't listen to him. Keep putting him off and be civil to him. Something's bound to turn up soon. Make us a mouthful of tea, like a decent girl, and put them things out of your head.'

When she had the tea wet she brought a cup in to Mary, sat beside her on the bed, and put an arm around her shoulder: 'Don't be fretting, Mary.'

Mary gave a forced laugh: ' 'Deed, Mother, I was very foolish. Sure it's all for the best.'

'Poor wee Peter will have a lonely bed to-night — God guard him,' and they sighed heavily and heard the wind stirring in the ivy. They spoke in whispers and they decided to go up on Sunday to visit him and cheer his heart.

But with Peter the first two days in the Home dragged by, and when he was out in the grounds the noises of the city were carried to him on the

46

wind: at 1.30 p.m. that loud, thick roar was Mackies' horn; and he thought of the men in their oily dungarees crowding slowly through the iron gateway and Frankie rushing up to school. Then he scanned the muddy fields around him, the mountain, and the red trams which he saw through the bare branches of the trees. Boys were playing football and in the cinder path in front of him he saw two big fellows peering into a hedge. They were laughing and one of them with bristles on his chin like a chestnut caught Peter by the arm and accused him of stealing a cigarette. Peter wrenched himself free: 'I haven't your cigarette!'

'You have it all right or you'd let me search you!'

'I haven't, I tell you!' and Peter put his hands above his head. 'Search me if you don't believe me.'

The big fellow put his hands in each of Peter's pockets and grinned malignantly, then he finally tapped the pockets and laughed:

'No, you haven't the cigarette. It's funny that I thought you pinched it.' And he put his arm round his companion's shoulder and went away laughing.

Peter sneered at them, but when he put his hands in his pockets his fingers touched a wet, viscous mass. He screwed up his nose as he turned his pockets inside out. In each of them were broken birds' eggs. He cleaned his pockets with grass, and the foul smell from the old unhatched eggs sickened him. He could hear the two big fellows laughing. He ran up to them and they waited for him behind two yew trees.

'What are you following us for?'

'You broke birds' eggs in my pockets.'

They laughed and held their sides.

'What's that?' one of them spluttered. 'You must be a sleepy noodle when you let a bird build a nest in your pocket.'

'I'll die if I laugh any more,' the other one said, and caught a branch of the yew tree to support himself from falling.

'I'll report the two of you!' and Peter turned to go away. The biggest fellow gripped him, twisted his arm, and pushed him against the yew tree.

He clenched his fist and pushed it under Peter's nose:

'Do you see that?' he grinned. 'Smell its strength!'

'I'm going to tell on you!' Peter persisted.

He tapped Peter on the chin, making his teeth rattle. Then he gripped him by the throat.

'Let me go!' and Peter tried to wriggle free. But the grip tightened on him.

'I'll tell! Let me go!' screeched Peter, kicking him on the shins. The big fellow struck at him fiercely and Peter fell to the ground. He lay for a minute and got up holding a hand over his right eye.

'If you tell on us I'll slit your throat,' and one of them took out a penknife and displayed the blade.

'Ps-s-t! Quick!'

The two boys hurried away when they heard footsteps on the path. Peter stood behind one of the yew trees and heard a group of boys arguing as they passed him. He felt his eye burning and swelling, and on his way back he saw an old nest hanging in tatters out of a hedge. If anyone asked about his eye he would say that he fell. But that night when he got into bed he decided that he would run away.

On Saturday there was to be a football match and he watched the visiting team arrive: a crowd of youths in grey caps, knotted mufflers, carrying their football boots in white paper parcels. Far behind them two small boys lugged a suit-case which contained the jerseys. Peter followed them to their pavilion and gazed in at them as they undressed and hung their clothes up on the nails. The air was cold and a sharp smell of embrocation came from the open door. Everybody seemed to be shouting and getting into one another's way:

'Give's a rub of that embro.'

'Has anybody a spare lace?'

'Hi, this jersey's as damp as hell!'

'How could it be damp? My oul' woman had them at the fire all week.'

'This jersey's damp too! The smell of it's like Ritchie's bone-yard.'

In about five minutes they ran out in a line on to the field where the Home boys were already waiting for them. Two small boys were left at the pavilion and Peter watched them playing marbles outside the door. He stood a short distance away from them and felt the frosty air smarting his bruised eye. More supporters for the visiting team were arriving and yelling themselves hoarse along the touchline. Two policemen came in to keep order and towards full time Peter saw caps being thrown into the air and fellows yelling: 'A penalty kick!' The two boys at the pavilion hastily put the marbles in their pockets and ran up to the field to see the penalty. Peter got to his feet, went into the pavilion, put a cap on his head, and found three pennies in one of the waist-coats. He slipped out again and when he heard the whistle blow for full time he joined the crowd that were running through the gate to the trams.

He sat on the tram until it reached the centre of the city. In a little shop he bought two buns, and wandered about the docks until dark. Then he made off for home, and furtively went up by the waste ground. It was dark; solid wedges of light slanted above every yard wall. For a moment he hesitated and wondered if he should sleep in the goat's shed. He stumbled against his father's hand-cart; The dog in the yard growled and as he approached the door it barked viciously. He rapped with his knuckles and spoke to the dog through the closed door. It ceased barking and sniffed expectantly around the jamb. The latch lifted in the scullery door and his mother's feet shuffled across the yard-tiles. The bolt scringed and she pushed

49

the dog to the side as she opened the door. The light from the kitchen shone out on him, and for a moment he stood in silence, the peak of the big cap to the side, his left eye blinking like a bird's.

'I'm back!'

'Peter, son, come in!' she said in a whisper, closed the door, and waited for him to speak.

'I — ran — away. There was no band and no shoes to mend and a big fella, bigger than Hugh, gave me a black eye,' and he took off his cap and turned his eye sideways to the light.

She clicked her teeth: 'My poor little son! You'll have to go back. The police will come for you. Your father will take you back. He'll go demented mad.'

He began to cry and she put her arm around his shoulder.

'Don't send me back and I'll go and work for my granny in the country and nobody'll ever know.'

She bit her lip and held him tightly: 'We'll see what your father will say.'

His three little sisters were sitting in a row on the sofa, shaking their washed legs, a white basin with soapy water below them.

'Oh-oh!' they shouted, and clapped their hands. 'Our Peter's home again! Peter's back from his holidays!' The mother hushed them and warned them not to mention to anyone that Peter was home, and as she stirred the fire under the kettle she listened to the three of them rhyme their prayers: 'God bless everybody in this house and please God make Peter a good boy . . . .'

A knock came to the front door and Peter bolted for the yard.

'No — no — in here!' and Kate opened the coal-hole door and pushed him in. It was pitch dark; the slacky coal crushed under his feet and trickled away from him. The air was stale and warm. He sat still and as his eyes grew accustomed to the dark he noticed chips of light in the door. He thought of cockroaches and spiders falling from the roof and he moved closer to the door. His mother opened it: 'It's all right, it was wee McCormick selling sticks.'

'What'd Peter go into the coal-hole for?' asked Lena, the eldest.

'Fwy fwas you in the coal?' imitated the youngest.

Nobody answered them and they giggled and hid behind one another's backs.

'You should all have been in bed an hour ago. And if there's any carrying on I'll be up with the strap. Go up quietly and don't waken the child.' They gathered up their rag dolls and with exaggerated quietness tiptoed up the stairs.

Later when everyone was in bed Kate and Johnny sat alone in the kitchen. They talked and argued about Peter, the trouble that he was giving them and the fine they would have to pay if they were caught harbouring him.

'If anyone saw him coming into the house we're caught. I think I should bring him back,' Johnny maintained.

'Och, the creature, his eye's a big as your fist. God only knows what'll happen him for running away. Sure, Johnny, we could send him to the country.'

The gas went out and they sat in the dull light of the fire. The lark stretched his wings and seed fell on to the floor.

Outside they heard a drunk man bawling out 'The Felons of our Land'. He dunted against the window sill and the words tumbled from him.

Johnny poked the fire. 'It's good to see somebody in good form and drink the price it is. That'll be Jackie McCloskey — his usual Saturday night's load up.'

Jackie went in next door and they could hear him singing, and Liza, his wife, trying to placate him.

'Whisht, Jackie, like a good man. You'll waken the neighbours. Let me take off your boots.'

51

'What do I care about the neighbours! Do the neighbours feed you? — No! Do the neighbours pay your rent? — No! Then what do I care about the neighbours. I'm going out now for a walk.'

'You can't go out, Jackie, in your stockinged feet; you'll get your death.'

'I'm going out in my bare feet. I'm as free as the winds of spring . . . A bird can't sing without seed; a man can't sing without a wee drop of drink.'

There was a stumble at the street door and a blurred mumble of words: 'Come in, Jackie, like a good man, I'm putting on the pan now.'

The door closed again and they heard the pan being lifted from the nail in the yard wall.

'God be good to that woman,' comments Kate. 'But she has the plague of a time with that man. She has the patience of a saint. If he landed home to me in that condition I know the supper I'd give him. A good bucket of water would sober him up.'

They fell silent as they watched the smoke-filled cracks in the coal, the spurts of a noisy flame, and heard the mice rustling about in the scullery.

Kate sighed: 'I'm thinking about Peter. Let Hugh take him on Monday to the end of the tram-lines in the handcart. He could fling a sack over him and nobody'd know the differs between him and a load of empty bottles. Then you could take him on the bar of the bike to his granny's.'

Johnny made no answer, and they heard Jackie going out into the yard and Liza trying to pull him back. The dog began to bark. A boot-brush, a hammer, and a washboard were flung over the Griffin's wall into the yard. Kate went out and picked them up.

'He's the heart scald of a man when he's drunk. And poor Liza will be in to-morrow apologizing for all this. "Kate," she'll say, "Poor Jackie loses his head when he's drunk. He's a good man. I tried to hide all the things that you lent me, but he searched up and down and yelled at me to be independent and not to borrow from the neighbours".'

'Don't take any notice,' cut in Johnny. 'He's harmless. To-morrow he'll be giving the children pennies and asking me to go for a walk with him.'

' 'Deed he's a kindly soul. Many's a time I think the best nature is in them that take a wee drop.'

Quietly she sat down and undid her hair. How would she get in the next two weeks? Peter was back, and then there was the rent man with the pencil behind his ear and his finger stuck in his black book: 'I'm afraid, Mrs. Griffin, I'll have to give you your notice.'

She started when Johnny spoke to her and the comb fell off her lap on to the floor.

'Maybe you're right about taking him to the country. We might get him hired out. His granny could never look after a fellow like that.'

Chapter V

Monday morning. Lena, Ann, and Rita came out of the house, closed the door, and made off up the street to school. Leisurely they passed along by the redbrick factory wall, Lena stopping now and again to clean Rita's nose with a piece of cotton rag which she carried in her schoolbag. Rita was finishing a crust of bread and she lingered behind the other two. They were very quiet and their canvas shoes made no sound as they trudged past the silent factory with its rusty wired windows and chalk-scrawled walls. Their faces were shiny, their hair neatly combed and bowed with wrinkled ribbon. A tall man wearing a raincoat approached them:

'Hello, children,' he greeted them cheerily, 'and you're going to school — the three of you? Isn't that good now? And you'll be in Second Book?' he added, addressing Lena.

'No, mister, I'm in Fourth,' she answered proudly.

'Fourth! Do you tell me that! You're a great girl — a grand girl! And little Mag, what Book is she in?'

The little girls giggled and Lena answered him: 'That's not Mag, she's Ann.' Ann smiled, held her head down and hid behind Lena's back.

'Well, now, sure I thought she was Mag. There's a penny for yourself and there's one for Ann,' and he handed two of them pennies and patted Rita on the head. Rita stared at him with her large black eyes and rubbed the crumbs from her mouth with the back of her hand.

'And your name?' he asked.

'Teeta!'

'No, mister, it's Rita — she can't say it right,' put in Lena with a shake of her head.

'Wait till I see have I a penny for Rita?' and he put his hand in his pocket and rattled his money. 'Just a few more left. There's one for you, Rita. And have you any brothers?'

'Two, mister,' Lena said. 'Frankie's in Sixth class and Peter was in the Home, but he's in the house and hides in the coal-hole when anybody knocks the door. And then there's our Hugh.'

'Oh, oh! I'll tell my mother what you said about Peter.'

'You mind your own business, Miss Ann. I'll tell what I like,' and Lena raised her chin saucily and smiled up at the tall man.

'Run along to school like good girls and don't be late,' and the nice gentleman patted them on the head and walked quickly away from them, stopped at the Griffin's house and rapped politely with his knuckles.

Kate opened at his knock and he walked in past her and stood in the middle of the kitchen floor.

'I'm a detective,' he announced. 'One of our men called here yesterday about your son, Peter. You denied knowing anything of his whereabouts. Since

54

he absconded we have grave suspicions that you are harbouring him.'

Kate turned pale and fidgeted with the dangling safety pins on her blouse. Johnny came out of the scullery with the towel in his two hands, soap in his ears, his braces trailing across the floor.

'Good morning, sir,' he said with ease. 'That's a playboy for you, and when I get my hands on him he'll not be fit to give anyone trouble again.' He unrolled his shirt-sleeves, pulled his braces over his shoulders, and nonchalantly put on his collar. The detective looked from one to the other and the lark began to sing.

'Maybe you'd sit down and wait for a while. He might land in on us this morning,' said Johnny, pulling on his coat, and brushing each sleeve with his hand. At that moment he saw Kate lift his bicycle clips from the table and for some reason all his brazen indifference left him. He combed his fingers through his hair and a lightness came over him.

'I'm afraid I'll have to search the house,' the detective said in a cold, officious voice. He stepped towards the coal-hole. Kate felt the things in the kitchen sway before her eyes, her heart pounded, seemed to stop, and she leaned on the table to support herself. The detective struck a match and in the corner of the coal-hole he saw Peter gathered up, concealed behind a newspaper. He pulled him out and Peter squealed.

'Aisy now,' said Johnny. 'He's not a criminal. Don't you begin to maltreat him!' And he railed fiercely at the Home for allowing a child of his to be beaten black and blue by two scoundrels.

'Is it any wonder we don't want to send him back! If he was your son you'd do the same. They needn't be putting a fine on me for shielding him, for I'm the man will take an action against the Reformatory for allowing an innocent child to get a bruised and

battered eye. A disgrace to civilization, I call it.'
But all Johnny's talk led to nothing, the detective
scribbled away in his book, and two weeks' later
Johnny appeared in court and was fined fifteen
shillings.

For a whole month Peter was allowed no visit.
Things went from bad to worse with the Griffins.
Every day Johnny lined up at the backs of the hotels
with his handcart, but he seemed to be black-listed
and his engagements were few. He tried to meet the
travellers coming off the boats in the mornings, but
here he was either forestalled or found that the
travellers' hampers were sent to the hotels in
advance.

As he walked with the greyhound at his heels up
through the park, past the wet seats and the bare
mournful trees, a deep gloom overshadowed him.
He sheltered from sleety showers in the draughty
summer house and listened to the pelt of the rain
on the glass roof or watched a few trees bleed their
last leaves. Gazing at the trees enmeshed with rain
or listening to the muffled sound of the wind in
the bare branches his mind would wander to the
country and he would walk away quickly to keep
from thinking and stand for a time looking into the
black river surging white over the stones or swirling
drifts of leaves amongst the twigs of a sunken
branch. But all these things stirred up in his mind
some remembered moment of his boyhood days in
the country and ravaged him with the bitterness of
regret. He thought of his mother: God knows she
was happy enough where she was and it would do
her no good to coax her into the city. He made up
his mind never to ask her again, but when he had
come in that evening from his walk his mind had
again changed, and foraging out an exercise book
from Frankie's schoolbag he began to write to
her.

'My dear Mother,

'I wouldn't write to you like this only I have to. We're in a very bad way — there's no nothing. Work is as scarce as good weather and only for Mary and Kate hemming handkerchiefs we would be out in the street. I didn't tell you this before for fear you'd think I was acting the poor mouth. But things are very bad and it's only you and your pension that could help us over the dregs of the winter when, we trust in God, things will improve. There's plenty of fine men walking the streets with nothing to do but they all think that after the New Year there'll be plenty of work. It's a long road that has no turning.

'If you come to stay with us for a while you will have a room to yourself and you can come and go as you please. I know how you feel about the country and the graveyard and the chapel two fields away, but it's not as if you were going to America or the Sahara. It's thirty miles from here to your house and that's nothing in these days with good motors and quick railways.

'I suppose you heard about Peter? He's in the Reformatory these past five weeks. God help him, he feels lonely at times and when Kate goes out to see him she can hardly get away from him.

'And I must tell you this: It never happened to any of us before to be living on Charity. But we had to do it. I filled in a card for St. Vincent de Paul Society and they sent a man round to find out how many we had in the house and how many we had working. They give us a grocery line for 3s. 6d. every week — it's not much but it helps to make ends meet. I wouldn't live on nobody's Charity if I could help it. There's a party up the street (no names, no pack drill) who's getting relief for the past three months and they don't need it. I call that robbing the poor and I'd add it to the seven deadly sins and make eight. It galls me to stay in on a Thursday night and wait for the two Vincent men coming

57

with their grocery slip.

' "Any change?" one will ask me.

' "No change, sir, no work," I answer.

' "Any prospects of work?" from the other wee man and he glances round the house and I always feel that he's prying for some clue that will knock my slip on the head. God forgive me if I am accusing the wee man in the wrong, for you could ring a bell for them — hail, rain, or snow they rap the door on Thursday night at half-eight. And it's the same mouthful of talk from them every week — just like a gramophone record.

'They were here last night and I thought at first that they were going to strike me off their books:

' "Somebody saw you trundling a handcart through Smithfield," says one.

' "That's true," says I, "for I was looking for work. It goes to my heart to ask for charity, sir. It's the first time anybody belonging to me had to do it."

'Then the wee man said: "There's a line for five shillings. You should apply for a bag of coal soon — Good night."

'Mary gets a little for hemming, but it isn't very much and she's nearly blinded into the bargain. She wants to get away to the nuns, but when she talks about entering a convent we don't encourage her. She's more useful to us here. But at the same time we wouldn't stand in God's way.

'You'll have no hens laying this weather with the fields in a slobber and no heat in the winds. Take care of yourself and write to us soon.

'Hugh hasn't done a hand's turn for months. He's not a bad fellow — a bit headstrong and carried away. He's courting a girl called Eileen Curran. She's a sensible lump of a girl, but she'll have a few grey ones before Hugh could marry her and make her comfortable. If he had money he'd smoke himself to death.

58

'Oliver had the measles. He's all right again, thank God, but one of his ears is beginning to run. Lena and Ann are in a little sing-song in the school and Mary made dresses for them out of the linings of old coats.

'I think that's all the news. It's not a bad place this to live in. There's fields a stone's throw away, a view of the mountain, and there's a river running at the back door. Maybe you'll come up and stay for a while.

'Good-bye now and write soon,
'Your loving son,
'Johnny.'

With a great flourish he drew a line under his name, read the letter over to himself, here and there inserting words which he had omitted. The he read it aloud for Kate's approval.

'I think, Johnny,' she ventured, 'you could have made a better fist of it. You could have told her what we had for our breakfast and dinner.'

Wouldn't the words about Vincent de Paul cover that?' he replied sharply.

'An old woman like her will know there's more applies for charity than what needs it. But have it your own way.'

He licked the envelope, closed it with a stamp of his fist, and went out to post it.

During the following days Kate watched for the postman, and when Johnny came in he always looked up at the mantelpiece to see if there was a letter for him. Nothing came and he tramped the streets with his handcart searching here and there for carrier's jobs, sometimes getting a job carrying old scrap iron, or conveying a piece of secondhand furniture for the dealers around Smithfield, or pushing to private dances large plants growing in small tubs.

In the evenings when the children had gone to

bed Liza McCloskey, the next-door neighbour, came in to chat with Kate. Kate always gave her a cup of tea in her hand, and one evening she asked her to read the cups. Liza brushed the crumbs from her lap and threw them into the lark's cage, then she put on her spectacles and held Kate's empty cup in her right hand. There was a moment's silence.

'There's a bit of tea-leaf there with a twist on it — that's a stranger coming to see you.'

Kate said nothing, she was thinking of the granny. Then after a pause she said: 'What else do you see, Liza?'

'There's something there like a ship or a motor car. You may be going on a journey.'

'The only journey I'll be going is up to the Workhouse. Do you see any money in it?'

'There's hasty news!' said Liza, peering into the cup with one eye.

'That'll be the notice to quit, I suppose.'

'Wait now. What's this? What's this?' and Liza turned the cup into another position and squinted at it thoughtfully. 'There's money, Mrs. Griffin. I can see it as plain as if it were in my hand. Look there, do you see that bundle of tea-leaves in the shape of a bag?' and she pointed with her little finger.

'Devil the happorth, I see,' commented Kate with a shrug of her shoulders.

'You haven't the cup-reading mind, Mrs. Griffin. There's money there as sure as an eye's in a goat . . . And here's a little disappointment at the bottom of the cup. But not much . . . And what's this at the top? A relation of yours coming in a hurry.'

'That'll do you, Liza. You've heard me talking about the old woman,' and she leaned forward in her chair and poked the fire to a flame.

'Now, Kate, that's not true. There'll be no luck if you doubt the tea-leaves. I've read cups for the past tewnty years and I've foretold many a person's

60

fortune.'

'Why don't you read Jackie's cup and see when he's going on the spree?'

'Och, God help him Kate, but he's a good, good man if he'd give up the bottle. It's ruining his health and there's not an insurance would take him on. His heart's bad since the day I married him. Did I ever tell you, Kate, how I met him?'

With her lips closed Kate smiled and listened with weary patience to Liza telling about her fateful encounter with Jackie.

'I met him at a jumble sale. The two of us were bidding for a pair of delf dogs and Jackie bid me out and got them. He must have seen how down-in-the-mouth I was for he slipped over and put the two dogs in my arms and then he asked to leave me home. I felt from the very first that he was a decent man and I fell in love with him and we were married within a month. Many's a time when I look up at the dogs on the mantelpiece I think of that jumble sale. Ach, Kate, there's no times like the oul' times.'

A thump on the wall from Jackie made her rise. 'I better go now, Missus, before he wakens your children with his thundering. He only got two days' work this week and he's as cross as two sticks.'

The following Monday when the children were at school Kate was finishing her washing when a gentle knock brought her to the door. She opened it and in walked two bailiffs, and before she realized what was happening they had opened the back door and had carried out the chest of drawers to the yard.

'Give us to the end of the week,' Kate pleaded with them. 'My man is promised a few days' work and we'll pay up the arrears right away.'

'It's not our fault, Missus,' one of the bailiffs assured her. 'We have our orders to carry out. This is our job and if we don't do it we'll be sacked.'

She went to the back door and looked over the waste ground for Hugh. There was no one about.

One of the bailiffs was backing the horse closer to the door and she saw how the wheels cut into the cinders and the clay. She hurried up the back and saw all the doors closed. Clothes swayed on the lines and she stooped below them and stood on the river-bank looking over at young men, in their shirt-sleeves, playing football. She waved to them, but they didn't see her. She came back to her own door. Already the bailiffs had the chest of drawers on the cart, pushed well to the front. They brushed past her, carrying things under their arms. For a minute they would stand with their arms folded, cogitating, and disputing about the most suitable position for each article.

'Put the mangle in the middle! It's too heavy for the back!' one said as he threw his coat over the shaft of the cart.

Kate came into the kitchen and saw on the floor a heap of old clothes, collars, ties, and jerseys that had been tossed out of the chest of drawers.

She went out to Liza's, rapped the door, but got no answer. The street was empty. She banged the knocker and hammered with her knuckles. Lisa wasn't at home. A little girl passed with a jug in her hand and Kate called to her:

'Run round to Eileen Curran's like a good girl and tell our Hugh to come quick! Tell him the bailiffs are here. Run hard!'

The loud knocking had roused a few of the neighbours and they put out their heads and Kate ran up to them, shouting in a husky, agitated voice to help her. Back again she came to the house, out to the yard, and over to where the young men were playing football. She called out to them, pointing to the cart and the horse, and the two bailiffs carrying out the sofa. Hugh wasn't amongst them, but when she came back he ran into the kitchen with his cap in his hand. With closed fists he confronted the bailiffs, but they ignored him and went on working quietly, filling up spaces with pots and ornaments and re-arranging the heavier articles. Back-doors were opening, and women were gathering in groups, their heads nodding, their voices rising in anger. Across the river the young men still played.

A rocking-horse which Frankie had won at a raffle was carried out and when the bailiff placed it on the ground it began to rock, its silver stirrups catching the weak sunlight. In the summer-time nearly every child in the neighbourhood had had its photograph taken on the Griffins' rocking-horse, the father of the child standing behind the camera, cracking his fingers and making tweety sounds to make the child laugh. And now as the rocking-horse was being hoisted on to the clumsy pyramid of furniture a woman went over and caught one of the bailiffs by the arm:

'For God's sake, Mister, leave them the rocking-horse!'

The bailiff mildly smiled, and Hugh caught him fiercely.

'Let go at once, young man, or I'll send for the police,' the bailiff said to him.

Hugh turned and raced over the bridge to the young men. They had stopped playing and they gathered round him, unrolling their sleeves. They could see the groups of women on the waste ground, the clothes on the lines, the horse and cart. One of the bailiffs was throwing a rope, and they saw it uncoil, wriggle and fall over the rickety pile of furniture.

In groups of three they crossed the river and converged on the cart from three directions. The bailiffs pretended to be unconcerned and one of them struck a match on the wheel of the cart, lit a cigarette, took his coat from the shaft, and slowly put it on.

Hugh approached him: 'Throw off your coat and throw off that furniture!'

63

The man straightened himself and eyed Hugh with a half-cynical leer: 'This is our work, young fella. Be careful or I'll send for the police!'

Hugh's hair was disarranged, his face pale, his black eyes very bright. The bailiffs tried to reason with him, gesticulating with their hands, emphasizing the honesty of their hard-earned money, and confirming their rights by producing many printed documents. Hugh took one of the documents and read it slowly.

Suddenly there was a cheer. The horse was unloosed and with jingling traces and men yelling it galloped up the fields. The shafts fell heavily to the ground.

'We'll get the police!'

'No, you'll not!' said Hugh, and a few of his comrades caught the bailiffs' arms, twisted them, and held them locked. The ropes that bound the pile were cut, and presently men and women were running back and forth to the house with the furniture. Soon the cart was cleared and one fellow sprinkled it with oil from the lamp and set it ablaze. The shafts were lifted and the blazing cart pulled towards the shelving river bank. With a cheer they gave it a wild push and the cart tumbled on its side into the river, one of the wheels revolving rapidly.

'There'll be trouble over this, Hugh,' the mother was saying, sitting quietly on the sofa, and looking at the bundle of old clothes.

Hugh was breathing quickly, his jaws sunken, his black hair in strands about his face. His fingers trembled.

'We couldn't do anything else but burn the cart. The fellows are collecting money for us round the doors and it'll help to satisfy the rent-man till things improve. We must fight to live. We paid our way when we had money and when we had work.'

He stood with his back to his mother, looking out of the window, one hand on the ledge. Women were talking to one another from their own doors and now and again they cast nervous glances down the street. He saw them withdraw, close their doors, and stand at their upstair windows. The police must be coming; and without consulting his mother he rammed home the bar in the front door, came back to the kitchen and pulled down the blind. The door was knocked.

'I'll open it, Hugh,' the mother rose to her feet. 'The easy way is the best way. Don't do anything rash, for the love of God.'

'Don't open it! Get up the stairs and lie quiet and they'll go away.'

Knocks came again to the front door and the back door simultaneously.

From the window he peered down into the street and saw the shiny peaked-caps of the policemen and the bowler hats of the bailiffs. The policemen heaved against the door and it creaked on its hinges.

'Open, Hugh, for God's sake! They'll burst it open.'

'I'll not. Let them burst away!'

He could hear people booing and he knew that from all the streets around crowds were gathering. The police hammered at the door with their batons; then a shower of stones rattled up the street, followed by cheers and shouts: 'Let the house alone! Let them live!'

The police charged; feet thundered past; doors clashed and women screamed. Hugh pulled up the window and looked out. The police were running heavily and ungainly, their yellow batons raised to strick. Suddenly they stopped and turned round. Hugh withdrew his head, and the falling window entrapped on the outside a tail of the yellow curtain.

'Hugh! Quick!' his mother shouted from the backroom. 'There's a peeler on the yard wall.'

As he jumped down the stairs to bar the scullery

door he heard the policeman drop on to the tiles in the yard. They arrived at the door at the same time; the policeman lifted the latch and Hugh leaned against the door from the inside. His rubber-soled shoes screeched on the floor. The huge weight of the police-man bulked large on the outside and his heels pressed into the ridges on the uneven tiles of the yard. He heaved with great force. The door opened slightly. Then it snapped viciously as the policeman lifted his right heel to place it in a deeper crater in one of the tiles. He turned sideways, putting his right shoulder to the door, holding his baton in his left hand ready to prod it between the jamb if the door opened again. Hugh spread his feet wide apart. He scringed his teeth and gathered his strength to ram home the bar. The door creaked, opened a few inches, and he saw the blunt nose of the baton levering against the jamb. Gradually the space widened, and with a last effort Hugh pressed heavily, then quickly he let go, and the policeman fell in a heap on the scullery floor. Hugh raced to the front door and as he made a dash for the street a policeman stuck out a foot, tripped him, and he fell face downwards on the kerb. Three of them gripped him and pulled him to his feet. There was a gash of blood on his mouth.

'I'll go quietly,' he said. But already they were dragging him away from the house.

'Let me get my coat,' he shouted. Turning his head he saw the bit of the curtain sticking out of the window.

'Come on! Your coat will be brought to you in the barracks.'

At the far end of the street youths stood in groups, and here and there women waved to him and children booed the police.

Chapter VI

The postman brought the news of the attempted eviction to the granny. She was coming out of the unheated chapel where she had been to morning Mass and was now standing on the worn step of the door looking at the white headstones that stretched out on all sides of her. It was a wintry morning and behind her came the burnt smell of snuffed candles and the pad of the altar boy's feet as he went to and fro from the sacristy. Two fields away she could see her thatched cottage and the smoke coming from the square chimney. The thought of the lighted fire made her move from the church door and she hurried over the wet grass to her people's graves, said prayers for their souls, and made off on the road for home. It was there the postman overtook her.

'Did you see the morning's paper?' he asked as he hopped off his bicycle.

'I gave up that foolish habit when I got married fifty years ago.'

'Be cripes,' says he, 'but there's something in this paper, photo and all, that'd make your heart rise,' and he opened out the paper and showed her a photograph of a street littered with stones and another picture of a four-wheeled cart lying on its side in a river.

'They did that!' he continued, giving the paper a smack.

'Did what?' she answered him puzzledly.

'Your friends! Johnny's son — when he bate the bailiffs black and blue.'

'What are you trying to tell me, Luke? You're worse than a child that's seen a runaway horse.'

'Ah, blazes to you, do you not recognize Johnny's house there marked with an X?' and he pointed with his thumb at the picture. 'That's where they bate the bailiffs and stoned the peelers. Johnny's eldest son did it. He's arrested! You should be proud of him. There's great stuff in him to stand up to the peelers the way he did.'

'And where'd the bailiffs come from?'

'Be cripes, didn't they try to put your Johnny out of his house?' and he stretched out the paper again and showed her the big print of the heading.

'Read it out to me, I haven't my glasses. No, Luke, come up to the house and get a bit of a heat from the fire and you can read it to me in comfort.'

The hens and the white cat clustered about her feet as she put the key in the door. The postman leaned his bicycle against the wall and stamped his cold feet on the stone floor of the kitchen:

'Be cripes, that's a hardy morning', and he gave the sods of turf a prod with his foot and sent sparks up the wide chimney. 'My feet's frozen riding that bike.'

The old woman closed the door and the grey ashes on the hearth rose in a whirl and flickered over the lid of the singing kettle. She pushed back the red cloth that cowled around her head and sat down on a low chair beside the postman. With great relish he read out the news, interspersing his reading with flavoured phrases of his own: 'Youth holds door against three policemen . . . Armed with poker makes daring dash for liberty . . . Women join in the fight . . . Police overpowered . . . But reinforcements arrive . . .'

The granny sitting at the fire listened to him rubbing her withered hands together and casting a glance now and again at the dresser where she saw Johnny's last letter sticking out of a tumbler.

'I didn't believe him,' she mumbled abstractedly.

The postman pushed his cap to the back of his head: 'You don't believe it, did you say? Well, then, I'll read no more. I'm wasting my time,' and he folded up the paper and made to rise.

'Stay, Luke, stay like a good man. Read on. I

believe every word of it.'

'My throat's a bit dry. Give us a drink of water like a decent girl,' and he eyed her smilingly, as she opened one of her trunks and produced the black bottle.

'I couldn't offer you spring-water a morning like that — it'd give you a scunder. I'll soon lift the dryness from your throat,' and she spoonfulled sugar into a bowl, poured out poteen from the bottle, and scalded it with water from the kettle.

The postman turned sideways to the window, crossed his legs, and began to read again, shouting it out as if she were deaf. When he took the warm bowl in his two hands he held it out like an offering: 'Here's to the Griffins! You should be proud of your grandson! There's great blood in him!'

She spoke little, answering him now and again with nervous nods of her head. Her hands were restless, and she stretched for the tongs and lifted every bit of turf that had fallen from the core of the fire. She put the tongs back and her right hand plucked at the loose skin on her throat. ' 'Tis terrible hard times to be living in,' and she pulled the red cloth over her grey head, put her hands in her sleeves, and nodded her head like one tottering off to sleep.

The postman shook the bowl to dissolve the sugar at the bottom, finished the dregs with a sigh of satisfaction, and wiped his mouth with his sleeve. He noticed the disconsolate look on the old woman's face and he put his arm on the back of her chair: 'Don't you worry about Hugh, Mrs. Griffin. He'll get off with a caution if he gets a good solicitor to defend him. Now, I know a . . .'

'Listen here, Luke,' she interrupted, and he saw that she was fumbling with her own thoughts. 'Send a wire to Johnny. Say that they can expect me to-morrow,' and she went into her room and got a shilling to pay for the telegram.

She stood at the door as the postman mounted his bicycle and rode off along the wet-black road. She gazed forlornly at the bare hedges and the cold-looking sky.

'God forgive me,' she breathed aloud, 'for not believing Johnny — he was always a great one for the truth.'

Above the hill in the demesne a rip came in the clouds and she saw the silver spokes of the sun stretch towards the earth, flicker for a moment, and disappear. The air became colder, and she turned to go into the house, stopped, put her hand to her ear and heard over the bare country the rumble of the morning train as it sped over the bridge at Toome. She set her clock on the dresser to the right time, bolted the door, and commenced to pack her two trunks. All the morning she went about the house in a sort of gloomy stupor. She ransacked drawers that smelt heavily of camphor, and as she turned up brooches or clothes that reminded her of her youth she would stand for a while in a kind of fretful daze, then suddenly start and look at the clock tick-tocking on the dresser. In one drawer she found an old checked schoolbag which had belonged to her children. In it there was a painted rubber ball, a pencil, a jotter, and two thin books. She took the ball in her hands and the paint fell off in flakes and the perished rubber crumpled like kneaded dough. The books smelt of damp, the leaves rust-stained from the wire clips. She blew gently to unloose two leaves that were stuck together and saw the names of her children written in studied, characterless handwriting: Michael Griffin, Patrick Griffin, Johnny Griffin. With a finger in the book she bent her head: 'God have mercy on the souls of Michael and Patrick! Two good sons . . . The very best . . . Life is short, but a great deal happens in it.' A spider ran out between the leaves of the book and fell on to the floor. She read some

70

of the poems and then reproached herself for wasting her time. She put the books back in the bag and dragged her two trunks out from the wall. Behind them swathed in cobwebs and white ash she found a thimble, buttons, and a darning needle.

The hens pecked at the window and she went out to feed them; and in the evening she walked to her neighbour a quarter of a mile up the road and arranged for them to take over the fowl until she came back from the city.

The next morning she was up early and got ready her two trunks which she intended to take with her. She swept the floors and covered the delf on the dresser with brown paper. She hooked the blinds to the two front windows, and the house became very quiet — death-like. The fire had fallen to a mound of ash and she made no move to put on more turf. She went into the room. Her feather-tick was looped over the rail of the bed and on top of it there glinted naphtha flake. She dipped a piece of palm in the holy water stoop at the door and sprinkled the room. It was a drag on her to leave her house and when she looked through the window at the back, at her little field and the trees that sheltered it, the loneliness of leaving filled her with grief. She would clasp and unclasp her hands, dodder about, mumbling to herself: 'The break-up of a home! It is worse than death!' When she was a young girl she had heard an old woman shriek that out on the road, and now the reality of its message came into her mind, surging back and forth, and she kept repeating it in spite of herself, rhyming it like the fragments of a song almost forgotten.

'But I'll be back in the spring, please God, or the summer at the very latest . . . It won't be long going in,' and she tried to sooth her mind with the thoughts of her homecoming. But something else was also worrying her, something she could not put a name to. And when she asked herself what it was her mind went numb and an apprehensive feeling would irritate her. To keep from thinking she pulled out drawers which she had already tidied, and in one drawer she began to count pieces of brown paper and loops of cord which she had accumulated. Then she went out and looked up and down the road, but there was no sound or sign of the lorry which was to take her to the city. The road seemed bare without her hens and the house seemed dead, blinds on the two windows and no smoke rolling up from the chimney. She came in again and sat on one of the trunks in the middle of the floor, but the something that she was forgetting teased her mind, and she tapped her toe on the ground and rubbed her fingers with vexation. The rumble of a lorry shook the house and she made no move until the latch was lifted and the driver, a blustering dirty-faced fellow, came into the kitchen. He said nothing when he saw her swollen eyes, a white handkerchief in her hand, and her belongings on the floor.

While he hauled out the trunks she buttoned her boots, put on her black coat, and skewered her hat to her head with black-headed pins. When all was stowed on the van she had a last look round the house, took her stick, and locked the door. The white cat came out of the drain-hole at the byre and rubbed herself against the old woman's leg.

'I knew I forgot something,' she said to the driver. 'It was battering at my mind all morning — it was the cat. She'll have to come.' And she opened the door again and carried out a basket with a wicker lid. Into this they put the cat and tied the lid with cord. Then they were ready for the journey.

The driving seat was high up from the ground, and the driver had to put a box under the old woman's feet and haul her aboard. When she was finally seated, the basket on her lap, she felt as if she were on top of a hay-rick. Everything smelt of oil and grease, and she was sorry now that she had on her best Sunday coat. The driver's clothes were polished with oil and she sat away from him. But whatever way she turned there was grease; there were black finger-marks on the door and pasted on the ceiling were cigarette cards and transfers. She said nothing to the driver when he lit a cigarette and smiled at her with very white teeth. With a sudden lurch they started off.

The morning was cold and the sky threatening. In front stretched the hedgy road with its muddy holes of water and loose stones. The lorry jolted stiffly as if it had no springs, and when it bumped into a hole and splashed the water into the shough, she held on grimly to the seat with one hand and with the other hand she kept the basket balanced on her lap. She didn't see her neighbour wave to her as she passed or the hens flying hysterically from the front wheels, for she was eyeing with growing apprehension a wriggle of steam issuing from the radiator cap. Now and again she breathed gratefully when a flutter of cold air came through the open window and blew strands of her hair across her face. She tried to settle down, but as each familiar clump of trees or old house flashed past a faded melancholy would weigh upon her and she would close her eyes wearily, only to open them again when the lumbering lorry crushed over stones and sent them bouncing into the hedge. Suddenly she sat up and gripped the driver by the arm. 'Stop! Turn back! I forgot to close the door.'

The driver slowed down, flicked out a cigarette butt, and spat impatiently through the window.

'Don't worry about the door. Ye locked it, for I seen you with my own two eyes.'

'I did the first time, but not when I went back for the basket.'

'But I seen you!'

'Something tells me I didn't. Turn back or I'll

not be easy in my mind.'

'For God's sake, woman dear, content yourself. Sure I'd tell you no lie. I seen you come out with the basket' — and with his hands he gave a demonstration — 'and I seen ye planting the basket on the ground and I seen ye turn the key in the lock and then I seen ye try the latch and make sure the door was closed.'

'But that was the first time . . . Turn or I'll walk back. You're getting a good penny for the journey and, don't forget, I engaged you.'

With good-natured resignation he backed the lorry into the nearest gateway and raced back along the narrow road. She found that she had locked the door.

'Now who's right?' said the driver smiling at her with his greasy face.

'It's a funny thing, but I don't mind locking it the second time.'

'Off we go for the last time,' and so fast did he start that she had to order him to take his time or he'd smash her trunks and the statue of St. Anthony which lay packed in straw in a wooden box.

She closed her eyes now and thought of Johnny and his children, wondering if they would be ready for her and if Luke had sent the telegram. She would stay a few months in the city and then a card to this lorry-man would bring her home again. The thought quelled the fretfulness in her mind and her mood changed to one of bright expectancy.

The Griffins, too, were excited and were eagerly awaiting her. All morning the children were awake and shouting: 'Our granny is coming to-day!' But they cried without success to get staying from school.

Mary's room was swept and washed, and the square of linoleum that lay at the kitchen fender was placed in the room to take the bare look off the boards. The air in the room was fresh and cold;

74

the window was propped at the bottom with a stick and when the door opened the draught sent the cotton curtains streaming like bannerettes. Johnny had sawn pieces off the wooden legs of the bed and under one which he had made too short he had hammered a wedge of wood. The picture of St. Patrick, crozier in hand, was installed at the foot of the bed, and at the head, nailed to the blue-distempered wall, was Mary's black crucifix. Mary had freshly lacquered the fireplace and in the grate she had placed a green frill of fan-shaped paper. She intended to drape the wooden rails of the bed, but Kate dissuaded her; 'It would make it too much like a wake-house and she might take a grudge and go home in no time. We must be careful, daughter.'

When everything was ready, Johnny, with a hammer in his hand, and Kate, with a towel over her arm, surveyed the room — the cool heaviness of the checked quilt, and table with its yellow basin, pink jug, and new cake of soap lying on a saucer.

'Fit for a Queen!' commented Johnny and put on his coat. 'I'll take the dog for a walk for he hates strangers.'

Frankie who had been kept from school was sent out to the street to keep a sharp look-out for his granny. He was tired of waiting and out of boredom tried to count the blue slates on the roofs of the houses on both sides of the street. When he would go whimpering into the kitchen his mother would jam a piece of bread for him and order him out again.

The children came out of school and Lena, Ann, and Rita were made take Oliver in his go-car to the Dunville Park where they would have shelter from rain and be out of all danger. Once or twice Frankie ran to the top of the street and came back again shouting into his mother: 'She's not going to come and I'm going to play.'

His mother would plead with him: 'Stay for another wee while. Something tells me she'll be here any minute now. I trust in God, son, she's met with no harm.'

'If she's not here before the lamplighter I'm going to play.'

He stood at the window-sill, a wry face on him, and began to make a ball out of papers and a handkerchief. The pamp of a horn made him turn and he saw a lorry amble up the street, the driver with his head stuck out watching the numbers of the doors. Frankie threw down his ball and rushed in: 'Mother, here's my granny now!'

'Glory be to God and my face dirty!' And she ran to the scullery and gave her face a wipe with the cloth. Frankie came to the door and saw his granny descending backwards from the seat in the lorry, the driver helping her to the ground. Kate hurried out: 'Thank God you're landed for my mind was sore tormented wondering if you had met an accident.'

With a pained expression the granny straightened her back: 'I'll not forget that journey-and-a-half till the day I die. I'm done to the wide world. Every bone in my body is achin' and my poor head . . . .'

'A nice cup of tea will soon lift your headache,' and Kate put an arm around the granny's shoulder and helped her into the house away from the prying eyes of the neighbours who were now peering out from behind their curtains.

Children were clustering around the lorry and clinging on to the back. The engine was hissing, and steam and water dribbled from all parts of it.

'Get us a bucket of water,' the driver was saying to Frankie. And when he came out with it he asked him to give him a hand with the trunks.

'She's a lively one that granny of yours,' he continued. 'She nearly had us in the ditch the way she grabbed the wheel. And she thought the old bus was going to blow up.'

Frankie stood on top of the lorry and lifted the wooden box containing St. Anthony's statue.

'It's not once or twice I had to look at him on the way in,' smiled the driver. ' "I tell you," she says, "I hear delf breaking." And when I got out to look there was Toni as peaceful and snug as if in a cradle.'

Presently the luggage was carried in, and when the lorry had roared out of the street with the dogs barking after it, the granny sat on the bed and launched into an account of the journey, stopping now and again to look round the room, while beside her stood Kate watching closely to see if her eyes registered approval.

'My poor feet is tortured,' she complained, stretching out her tight-fitting buttoned boots.

Kate stooped and, with studied gentleness, removed each boot. 'Thank God for that relief,' sighed the granny, and lay back on the bed. Kate got her an old pair of carpet slippers, helped her off with her coat and hat, and led her out to the kitchen where the rocking-chair with a green cushion awaited her.

Frankie sat on the fender and gazed open-mouthed at his granny, at her wrinkled face and the pink scalp showing through her thin hair. There was a black shawl about her shoulders held together with a gold brooch, and as she placed her feet on the fender and kept rubbing her hands she asked him about Peter, about his school, and what he intended to be when he grew up.

'What way do you like your tea — strong or weak?' Kate asked cheerily.

'I like it thick,' the granny nodded and poked the fire.

'That's right — make yourself at home,' said Kate. 'And there's Frankie can crack to you like an old grandfather.'

While waiting for the tea to draw Kate praised the lovely flawless stitch in the granny's shawl: 'And you tell me you knit that yourself! There's our Mary and the nuns is always talking about the great hands she has, but she couldn't knit like that. What paper did you get the pattern in?'

'Out of my own head,' the granny answered, proudly patting her shawl.

She preferred taking her tea where she sat, the cup and plate resting on the hob beside her. Frankie was sent out to look for the children, and Kate whispered to him to keep them away from the house for at least an hour.

After the tea she coaxed the granny to rest for a while on top of the bed. And later when the children were washed and beribboned they were marshalled into the room to see her. When they were put to bed and the house quiet she came out and sat on the rocking-chair and listened to Johnny telling about the bailiffs and Hugh's two months' sentence. Mary quietly stitched away, pausing occasionally to add a word to the conversation, and then gathering all her hopes together she sighed for the day when she could afford to leave for the convent.

Chapter VII

The granny would waken in the early hours, turn her head towards the blindless window, and see between the curtains the clouds of night or hear the ivy leaves brushing mournfully against the pane. From under the pillow she would grope for her beads and try to tire herself with prayer, but a striking clock would invade her mind and sweep away the blurs of sleep. Fully awake now she would listen with impatient dread to the strike of other clocks in the neighbouring houses: how different they all were — as different as human beings. One would chime hurriedly, another slowly and deliberately, and then their own clock in the kitchen would give out a husky, gritty strike like the cough of an old man. Why couldn't they all strike together? And there was one that struck seven times when the others were striking three. Their irregularity irritated her, and time and again she would cover her head with the clothes, but the sound always baffled her, swinging into her mind and nagging it to a peevish wakefulness.

At times she blamed the air of the city for her sleeplessness and sometimes accused the bed. The horsehair mattress was hard and lumpy and refused to sag or mould itself to her shape. At home she sank into her own feather tick which drooped under her like an old hammock. Lying awake she would think of that feather tick, the sleepy hum of the wind in the hedges, and the absence of chiming clocks to measure out for her the inexorable drag of the night hours. If only the brush of the leaves on the pane were anything but ivy it may have solaced her mind, but ivy she disliked and she would see that Johnny stirred himself and cut it down. Sometimes when the cold daylight was sifting through the darkness her eyes would droop and she would doze over till the clash of a door or the lark singing in its cage would startle her.

When the children had gone to school Kate would call to her and have her tea and toast warming on the hob. The granny would come out slowly, the red flannel about her head, the black shawl on her shoulders, and take her place on the rocking-chair at the side of the fire.

'How'd you sleep last night?' Kate would ask solicitously.

The granny would nod her head and rock the

chair with her two hands: 'Och, I didn't bat an eyelid the whole night.'

'Is your bed warm enough?'

'It's not that. The bed's hard and it's all lumps into the bargain.'

'Horsehair mattresses is all the style now. But if you don't like it, maybe Johnny could get your own fetched up from the country.'

'He'll just leave it where it is. It'll not be long now till I'll be back again,' and she would stretch out a hand and take a long draught from her mug of tea.

She would shrug her shoulders, cower into the chair, and complain about the cold: 'Why don't they have the fires lower down and not stuck up under your chin where a body doesn't need the heat?' She would lift the poker, plunge it between the bars of the grate, and rake the fire vigorously. Ashes would rise in a cloud and alight on the brass ware on the mantelpiece or the shining fender. At such times Kate stemmed her tongue, piloting the talk away from danger, and replenishing the mug with good strong tea. But when the tea was not to her liking she would fling down the poker with a rattle, go into her room, and give the door such a bang that it shook the delf on the shelf. Her arm-chair would continue to rock and the cat would jump on to the seat and curl itself on the warm-crushed cushion.

'She'd break the patience of a saint,' Kate would say to herself. 'But please God a good steady job will turn up soon for Johnny.' And pulling on her hat and coat she would set off to buy something for the dinner.

When Kate had gone out the granny stood at the window — or at the door if the morning were fine — and took stock of all the neighbours who passed by. Every morning an old man in a bowler hat left the house opposite, his hands in his overcoat pockets, his feet shuffling along the ground. He always had his head down, and often she would see him stoop, lift a piece of paper blown in at the edge of the kerb, examine it and sometimes put it in his pocket. Another door would open and a bent old man with a milk jug in his hand would trail off down the street. His elbow was out of his coat and the granny often pursed her lips with scorn and said to herself: 'It's a poor sort of a woman that'd let a man walk the streets of Belfast with a hole in his sock and no elbow in his coat. Lazy good-for-nothing clarts!' From the same house a young man in his shirt-sleeves would come out with a basin of steaming water in his hand, climb on to the sill, and clean the windows with a yellow chamois. From where she stood she could hear the squeaks of the dry cloth on the pane and see the steel shods on his heels as he knelt upon the sill.

Sometimes after cleaning the windows he sharpened a knife on the sill, and as she watched the prickled sparks and the worn scallops on the stone she wondered how long it would be till the sill was worn down like an old shoe. She would be dead then — long dead. And she remembered the curve on the chapel doorstep in the country — hundreds were dead now who had trodden across it. Everything was wearing down — that was life. A man was worn down by work and worry. How many coffins she had seen borne to the graveyard and were now indistinguishable from the clay which had once been shovelled down on them. There was something then that didn't wear out — a soul. And she recalled words from her Catechism: 'What do you mean by saying the soul is immortal? — I mean that it can never die.' Well, if it doesn't die it must grow; it would grow with grace or twist and sour itself with sin. God help us all! And she sought for her beads in her pocket. The man would cease sharpening his knife, lick his thumb, rub it along the edge of the blade, and with a shake of his head wink over at the granny and close the door behind him.

Beside his house was a little sweet shop: CHOCO-LATE printed in white porcelain letters on the pane, the H and T now missing. In the window were boxes of sweets, a plate with buns, and hanging from a brass rail cards of soothers, stomach powders, and Beecham's pills. Many a time a bare arm would stretch over the brass rail, grip a fistful of sweets and rattle them into the scale for the granny. Sometimes she bought for herself snuff or peppermints, but the hard sweets she secreted in an inside pocket for the children.

Another regular visitor to the shop was an elderly woman who lived in the house to the right of it. She was notorious for borrowing money which she never paid back, and Kate warned the granny to have little truck with her and not be deceived by her plausible manner. Her husband was lazy and studied night and day the *Sporting Chronicle*; and at one time he had to lie in bed for three days, because he had forced his wife to pawn his complete and only suit in order to back a 'dead certainty'. Many's a morning the granny saw her leave the house with a brown parcel under her coat, return without it, and emerge again with a jug or a basket. The granny was distant with her, but she grew to like her nearest neighbours: Liza McCloskey and 'Stick' McCormick. 'Stick' was a small delicate-looking man, his knees slightly knock, and his clothes hanging loosely on him. His wife was an enormous buxom woman, shaking with fat and good humour. They had ten children, some of them always crying. 'Stick' specialized in gathering empty boxes, and all morning the granny could hear him whistling as he chopped sticks in the yard. Later in the evening his eldest boy came out with a home-made cart filled with sticks which were tied up in penny bundles.

When he called at the Griffins the granny never refused to buy from him, and sometimes gave him a sweet for himself if he spoke to her civilly and answered all her gossipy questions. In this way she got to know the neighbours by name, and later she learned that the man in the bowler hat had once found a pound note in the unswept litter in the street and ever afterwards had drooped his head and walked along with a shuffling gait.

But there was one house and its inhabitants which irritated her with its air of mystery. Two spinsters lived in it, their dark green door usually closed, the brass knocker and letter-box always shining. Every Friday morning the door would open wide and a pram, laden with bundles and covered with a rain-proof sheet, would be pushed out, and behind it would appear the two maidens, stiff and grand in their tight-fitting clothes. On the window-sill they would place a milk jug with a saucer resting on the top. If the granny were standing at the door as they approached, she would go inside and from behind the curtain she would stare after them in wonderment and mystery. On Friday evenings they would come home, take in the milk-jug from the window, wheel in the pram, and close the door. No one could tell where they went, where they worked, or what they did all day.

It was Frankie who was the granny's confidant in all these matters, for it was he who conveyed to her the local news and it was he who got out early from school on a Thursday afternoon to accompany her to the post office while she drew her old age pension. He liked pension day, for she usually gave him a few pence for himself, but he was annoyed if, when he arrived from school, he would find her washing clothes and crouching over the bath on the chair. The washing made her cranky and once when Mary and Kate had intervened and pleaded with her

83

to allow them to wash for her she glared at them: 'While I'm in this house I'll keep my independence. Nobody ever washed as much as a dish cloth for me in their lives and they'll not do it now.'

To do her washing she usually hauled out a stool to the middle of the kitchen floor, put the gas-ring on top of it, placed a penny in the gas meter and boiled her bucket of clothes until the meter had released its quota of gas.

One Thursday Frankie arrived from school to find the bucket on its side, suddy water bubbling across the floor, the stool on fire and the gas-ring blazing away. His granny had gone to the yard for the bath and when she came in and saw him scooping up the water with his hands and flinging it over the blazing stool, she blamed him for up-setting the bucket on her, and ordered him to his two knees to wipe up the mess.

'I didn't do it!' he kept whimpering as he wrung out the floor-cloth.

'You did. You tumbled the bucket when I was out in the yard. It surely didn't walk off the ring by itself and topple on its head.'

'I didn't do it!'

'Don't answer your granny back! Remember what day it is!' and she opened the scullery door to let out the choking smell of burnt wood and soapy water.

She went into her room, stabbed on her hat with three hat-pins, gripped her stick, and was ready for the road.

Sulkily he walked with her out of their own street With its low red-bricked houses. It was a sluggish, misty day. The pavements were damp, and as the granny felt the hard, unyielding ground under her feet she thought of her little field in the country and the soft path to the well. He could feel her weight pressing him down. Then she stopped and prodded with her stick a piece of crumpled paper.

'Lift that!' she said to him.

He kicked it with his toe. 'It's only an oul' piece of tissue paper,' and he sniffed through his nose and tried to disengage his arm which she was holding.

'Now don't walk so fast, Mister Smarty! You're out with an old woman and not with Mary.'

They passed into another street of small houses, each with iron railings enclosing a garden wide enough to grow a hedge. Some had the patches covered with white stones or cement, others judging by the scraps of cloth nailed here and there on the wall had tried to train plants. They could see over the iron railings into the houses, seeing a man in his shirtsleeves reading a newspaper, a girl cleaning a range, or a child sitting on an upturned stool playing motors.

A young mother was cleaning a semi-circular space in front of her doorstep, and Frankie got red to the ears when the granny stopped and chatted with her. Her baby was crawling behind her and the granny admired it and gave instructions on the best way to wean it: 'Go slowly at first, daughter, and never give him hard food till he's fifteen months or it'll tear the lining off his wee bowels.'

'I'll do all you say, Missus,' the young woman replied, rubbing soap on her brush and winking furtively at Frankie.

'What do you call that party?' the granny asked when they were out of earshot.

'I dunno,' Frankie replied gruffly, and as they walked on she pestered him with questions about the passers-by.

He pretended not to hear her, and she pinched his arm: 'Are you hard of hearing, Frankie? You'll get no penny from me if you're not more sociable with your granny . . . Do you hear me?'

To his dismay she called into the chapel and there she went round the Stations of the Cross, he having to help her off her knees at each Station.

'She puts half of the old age on,' he thought to himself, though he hadn't the courage to tell her so.

After much genuflecting they were out again and off on the final round to draw her pension. The post office official, a thin man with tight lips, exasperated her. He kept her standing for a long time while he checked up his accounts, and then roughly taking her pension book which she had carefully folded in brown paper he viciously stamped it and tossed it back to her under the wire-meshed counter.

'The paper, please,' she asked, and without a word he picked it up from the floor, pushed it to her, at the same time looking coldly at Frankie.

'Why are so many of them post people so coarse-mannered, Frankie? God-a-God, son, you'd think the money was coming out of their pocket the way they order a body about with their perky manners — there's no kindness in them. I tell you, Frankie, there's big changes coming over the people now. They're not like the old ones. They're always in a hurry and no time for a chat. Och, there's no neigh-bourliness in the city. I think, Frankie, your oul' Granny will pack her bag soon . . . Come down with me till I change this note.'

Back home again she sat down on her chair and wearily stretched out her buttoned boots: 'Careful, son, careful,' as he unhooked the buttons and gripped a boot in his two hands. 'They have my poor feet scalded,' and she placed her parched feet on the cold tiles. Under her bed he got her house-slippers and carefully put them on for her.

'Just leave that hat and coat on the bed and I'll hang them up when I gather my breath. My poor heart's overwrought . . . And, Frankie, take the jug from the table in the room and get me a pennorth of milk in the wee shop and tell the girl to take threepence for snuff.'

He was soon back again and handed her two pennies change which she put in her purse. She got him to heat the milk in a saucepan and put a shake of pepper in it. He sat on the fender gazing up at her with meek expectancy and watching the sleepy droop of her brown eyes as she sipped the milk and crumbled a piece of bread on her lap. She ate and drank noisily, and her jaws moved in a strange mechanical fashion. When she had finished she brushed the crumbs from her lap and gave them to him to throw to the birds.

'Did you see is there lashings of baking soda in the tin?' she asked him abruptly.

'I forgot, Granny,' and he went into her room and brought out a small tin and rattled it. Recklessly she emptied the contents on to her palm and swallowed it.

'Ye better get me another pennorth,' and he eyed her as she delved into her pocket for her purse. She stared back at him; she knew what was in his mind, but she'd make him wait — help to control himself. When she was his age she hadn't everyone thrusting pennies into her hand; and anyway the children nowadays were spoilt: they were always looking for payment even if they brought you a cup of water.

He didn't like the way she was staring at him and he smiled at her with his lips closed and asked: 'Granny, why do you eat so much powder?'

'To kill my pains. Only for baking-soda you'd have no granny. And what'd you do then? . . . 'Deed, I suppose, you wouldn't care if I was under the clay to-morrow. Poor wee Peter would have cared.'

Frankie fidgeted and lifted her handkerchief which had fallen to the floor.

'I think I'll lie down on top of the bed for awhile and you'll get your mother to waken me about six,' and she got up stiffly from the chair and trailed into the room.

When he came back from the shop he put her tin of baking-soda on the table in her room and stood for a minute without speaking. She was breathing with deep weariness, her back towards him, her coat around her shoulders.

'Is that all the messages now?' he inquired politely, looking down at his boots with their shining eye-holes.

'Just a minute! Just a minute!' and she fumbled for her purse and squeezed two pennies into his hand. 'You're a good boy, Frankie. And some day the two of us will go to the country and I'll get you a donkey and cart for yourself.

He laughed nervously: 'But you said you'd buy a donkey and cart for Peter.'

'I'll buy two donkeys and two carts and you'll go to the moss and bring home the turf . . . And, Frankie, keep the children quiet when they come in from school and let your poor granny get a sleep, for I'm not long for this world.'

But when Lena, Ann, and Rita had come in from school Frankie was nowhere to be seen. They sat on the stairs and hammered them with a stick. They argued noisily over coloured pieces of cotton or glass beads, and later Lena conducted a choir.

'This place is like bedlam!' the granny groaned to herself, rose up from the bed, and came into the kitchen with her knitting in her hand.

The children got ready to play a 'school,' and when the granny had fixed on her glasses she would occasionally look over the top of them at Lena, smile wanly, and turn towards her knitting.

'Now children,' Lena was saying in a mincing perky voice, and began to clap her hands. 'I'll be the teacher and you'll be my class.' In a few minutes everything was arranged. The teacher came out of the scullery with an old coat of Mary's brushing the floor, a handbag tucked under her arm.

'Here's teacher,' Ann said. 'All keep quiet.'

The teacher entered, holding her chin aloft. She wrinkled up her nose and sniffed audibly: 'The air in this room is a little stuffy. Perhaps, Ann Griffin would open that window, please.'

The teacher carefully removed her coat and hat, bunched out her hair, and put a rag of a handkerchief up her sleeve. She propped the blackboard — the lid of a tea-chest — on the seat of a chair and threw the floor-cloth over the rung as a duster.

'Now girls, please take out your pencils and jotters. No talking,' and she gently clapped her hands again and pretended to write a sum on the blackboard. Ann sat on the stairs, the pencil pressing on her lower lip, her eyes raised to the ceiling in an affected attitude of deep thought. Suddenly she lowered her head and scribbled excitedly; at the same time Rita turned her jotter over and sat with arms folded.

The teacher with extreme delicacy scratched the top of her head with a pencil, smoothed her eyebrows with a licked finger, and with an exaggerated flourish looked at her wristlet watch. 'Pencils down!' she ordered and went round to examine the books.

The old woman burst out laughing, and the children jumped up and scrambled round her asking her what was wrong.

'I have something nice for all of you,' and from her pocket she took out a few sweets, picked off the paper that had stuck to them, and handed one to each with the same question: 'What do you say?'

'Thank you, Granny.'

'And I have something for you,' Lena said proudly, and from her schoolbag she foraged out a disused electric bulb which she had found in a bin. 'Mary uses one of them as a darner and you can take this one,' she continued, and got a sock with a hole in it from the cupboard and stretched the hole over the curved glass of the bulb.

'You're a kind girl, Lena, for remembering your granny . . . Run on out now and get the air about yourselves,' and because it was pension day she gave them halfpennies each, and when the house was quiet she relapsed into her chair, her needles clicking, her jaws moving.

On pension day she always sat up late at night and Johnny and Kate would sit with her, patiently waiting till she retired and the gas turned safely out. If she were in good humour she would call Kate into her room and count shillings into her hand, but if her mood were cantankerous she would say nothing about her pension till the following day. At this time Johnny, himself, was making a few shillings every week, buying a basket of odd delf in Smithfield, hawking it round the entries and exchanging a mug or a bowl for rags or scrap iron. But often he would complain bitterly to Kate: 'There's plenty of money to be made at it, but like everything else there's too many at it.' He contemplated buying a horse and cart and selling coal, but a coalman had discouraged him telling him about the bad times he had had collecting debt. 'It'd put you demented mad, Johnny,' he assured him. ' "Just leave us another bag this week and I'll square the lot in a few days," is what your customers will tell you. But do they square it? Not damned likely! They're off to another coalman while you'd wink. And mind you, Johnny, you can't feed a labouring horse the way you'd feed a dog. You have to look after him . . . Take my advice and don't get messed up with a coalcart.'

And at night when they had all gone to bed, the kitchen, with the lark asleep in its cage and the clock ticking, seemed to lose for ever the strain and strangle of noisy children and to plunge itself in a depth of peace. It was then that Johnny and Kate sat together — the gas turned out and the last dregs of a fire subsiding in the grate — no talk about his work, the children, and the old woman.

'She's discontented, Johnny. I don't think we can keep her any longer,' Kate had said one night after the old woman had retired to her room in a fit of silent anger.

'Can Mary do nothing with her?' Johnny answered. 'She should take an interest in her: take her to the market or up to Ardoyne and let her hear the Passionists or up to Clonard and let her hear one of them Redemptorists giving out on Death. She likes nothing better than to hear a good preacher.'

'Och, Mary is still talking about going to the convent. But when she mentions it I pretend not to hear her.'

'It'll wear off,' replied Johnny. 'It's like a girl's first love — all fancy and dreams and no depth in it.'

The fire shrunk to a dull red. Outside rain splashed from a broken spout and trindled down the grate. Footsteps hurried up the street; a door opened and shut.

'We'll have a full house when Hugh comes out,' and Kate went into the scullery for a cup of water to take up with her to the room.

'I suppose he'll be that well-mended he'll ate like a horse. If he could knock out a job I'd be contented in my mind.'

'Isn't there a stick factory somewhere for lads just out of jail?' she asked.

'I inquired about it, but its not for fellows like Hugh. It's a sort of reforming factory run by Vincent de Paul men. He'd never get in there — his record is too good.'

They laughed at that; and then they heard the creaks of the granny's bed as she turned in it. Johnny got up from his chair and quietly ascended the stairs.

Chapter VIII

The day that Hugh was released from prison the neighbours greeted him in the street: 'Welcome home again, Hugh. Fresh and well you're looking. Ye'd think ye'd been on a cruise.' Or 'A houl you, you didn't smoke much in jail.' Or 'Eileen Curran will be taking another notion of you. She's failed to scrapins since you went away.'

His clothes were too tight for him and Johnny presented him with the old tweed coat that Peter had got from the little woman the day he had cycled to Toome.

'It fits you like a glove,' said the old woman, taking his two hands and patting them gently. 'I'm proud of you.' He felt shy and awkward as he watched the cold, bony fingers caress the backs of his hands. When she raised her head he noticed tears in her eyes. He withdrew his hands and stepped back from her. She took a pinch of snuff and from under the green cushion she pulled out a long red handkerchief. He turned away, strode over to the cage, and made tweety sounds at the lark.

'Come over and sit beside me for awhile,' she asked in a quavering voice. He pretended not to hear her and from the corner of his eye he noticed her moving lips and her fingers tapping the arms of the chair. There was something about her that made him uncomfortable, and he wondered was it the smell of snuff, her husky cough, or the eternal fidgets of her fingers. 'Do you think he's well-mended?' Kate asked, aware of Hugh's sullenness. The old woman nodded, rocked the chair, and began to rake the ashes.

Hugh went out by the back door. The greyhound sniffed at him timidly, and then realizing who it was, licked his hands and barked joyously. The roof of the goat's shed was littered with stones which children had flung on top of it. Everything about the waste ground seemed strange to him, as if his mind were dazed. The round roof of the brick yard gleamed with fresh tar, and towards the archways of the kilns men with rolled-up sleeves and red dust on their trousers were wheeling barrows of clay brick, while others came to the edge of the river and tumbled barrows of ash down the shelving side, the dust rising in a cloud, thinning out and merging into the air. The wheels cut tracks in the soft mud and now and again one of the men would sit on the shaft and gaze into the flooding river. To the right of the brick yard, children were rooting amongst the piles of paper, tins, and bottles that sheered to the water's edge. Hugh saw Frankie squatting on his hunkers and putting sticks and cinders into his bucket, but he didn't call to him. He remembered himself as a boy collecting empty bottles and the day he found University examination papers and was astounded to read that it took three hours for one paper.

He hitched a stone over the bank and when the dog scrambled after it he ran off laughing to escape from him. He came out on to the street that led to Eileen Curran's. The pavements were wet, drab-looking, and even the look on the people's faces seemed subdued and inert. The air was frosty, and over the roofs of the houses the dusk was falling and gathering into doorways and entries. A few little girls rope-swinging from a lamp-post spoke to him: 'Mister, would you tie the rope further up till we get a better swing?' The word 'Mister' pleased him. He had grown stout during his term in prison; his cheeks were still pale though no longer hollow, his black hair clipped close, his shoulders broader.

The lamplighter with his yellow pole over his shoulder passed him and Hugh turned round to see the children scrambling to pull down the rope. He had knotted it too tightly. The children ran, and from the seclusion of an entry they jeered at the lamplighter as he cut the rope and stuffed it into his pocket. He lit the lamp and a halo of weak light spread itself into the air.

Eileen's door was open and Hugh stepped into the kitchen. Through the back window he saw her in the yard plucking clothes off the line. She was alone. Her fair hair was twisted up in curling rags, her arms bare to the elbow, and in her mouth were two clothes-pegs. Hugh hopped into the coal-hole and pulled the door behind him. He heard her coming in and heard the rasp of the starched clothes as she bundled them on the table. She pulled down the blind and lit the gas. She blew off flakes of soot from the stiff folds of the clothes and with her finger-nail scratched off a speck of dirt embedded in a pillow slip: 'It's not worth a body's while hanging out clothes in this place,' she sighed to herself. From the scullery she took an iron, shook out the heater, and pushed it into the heart of the fire. She stood waiting for it to redden. She was a small girl and always wore the highest of heels to make herself taller.

Hugh pushed open the door and tiptoed over to her; he put his hands over her eyes and she gave a frightened scream. 'Who is it?' he asked, not trying to alter the pitch of his voice because he had frightened her.

'Somebody with no manners,' she answered, endeavouring to wriggle free. He bent back her head and kissed her.

'Now who is it?'

'You put the heart out of me!' and then remembering about her curlers she snatched a handkerchief from the table and knotted it around her head. Her grey eyes were alive with anger, surprise, and delight.

'Are you not glad to see me, Eileen?'

'I am, but I didn't expect you round till the night. I should have known to keep the door locked,' and she stooped to peer between the bars of the grate at the reddening iron. He put his arm round her waist.

'Hugh, please, let me go till I get my smoothing done. They'll all be in on top of us any minute.'

'You get on with your work and I'll help you,' and he lifted down a porcelain match-bowl from the mantelpiece and placed it on the table: 'Isn't that what you rest your iron on?' With her lips closed she smiled at him and stretched out her hand. He took her in his arms and she leaned her head against his shoulder. Outside, a newsboy shouted the evening paper and a milk-cart rattled up the street.

'Look, Hugh, the heater! It's red hot!' With the tongs he gripped the glowing iron and skilfully manoeuvred it into the box-iron.

He sat at the table as she spread out the clothes and flicked drops of water over them with her fingers. She ran the iron stiffly across them, and as its boat-shaped snout devoured the folds the drops sizzled and a warm biscuity smell rose into the air. He saw her knuckles whitening as she pressed heavily on the handle of the iron and in its curved silvery sides he watched with boyish amazement the elongated contortions of his face. She packed the folded handkerchiefs to the side and he lifted one of them and placed its warm surface against his cheek.

'You're worse than any child,' she said to him as she turned over a white silk scarf; on top of the scarf he playfully put his finger and gradually withdrew it as the heater advanced.

'Now be careful if you don't want a right burn,' she said and leaned so heavily on the iron that the cutlery jingled in the table-drawer.

'Man, Eileen, it'll be a great day when you're smoothing my shirts like that.'

'That'll be a long time, Hugh,' she replied tonelessly.

'What makes you say that?' and he got to his

feet. 'If I get a job it'll not take me long naming the day.'

'Didn't we talk about all that before, Hugh? How when Mary was to go to the convent we could get her room and settle down. Now your grandmother has come and upset everything.'

He laughed bitterly: 'Well, that's the best ever I heard. Sure the old woman will be away back to the country before the end of the summer.'

'For goodness' sake don't make plans. I've seen too many of mine broken in smithereens by things I never thought of. No, Hugh, it's better to live week by week and not to hope for too much,' and as she folded a frock she held it under her chin.

'That's damned funny preaching talk. I'm afraid you've been going to the Custom House steps on a Sunday. Sure, how can anything be done if you don't plan — and plan in advance?'

'I know — I know! But there's something — I can't explain. There's something always ready to pounce and smash what you've made.'

He bit his under lip and squeezed her arm. 'You're tired,' he said, at a loss for a convincing reply. 'You've too much work to do for your pack of sisters; they're heaving it on to you because you're the youngest. But some day I'll lighten your load and you can crack your fingers at the whole crowd of them . . . I'll be round about half-seven and we'll go for a walk.'

When he left her house he was surprised at the thick darkness that had fallen. The windows at each side of the street were lighted, and here and there he could see the outline of a flower-pot on the blind or the shadow of a lace curtain. The angelus bell from Clonard was ringing, factory horns were blowing, and people were hurrying.

A gloom had come over his mind: that was a way for her to talk about the future — Don't plan too much! And what in God's name would you knock

96

out of this world if you didn't plan? He walked quickly, trying to tear from his mind the web of twisted thoughts or wither them in the distractions of the street. Workmen passed him, smelling of oil and grease. It's a great pity he didn't serve his time at some trade — he might have had a constant job now and a good enough wage to set up a house for himself and Eileen. There was something after all in what she said: not to plan too much — there's too many people living on dreams and some of them live on nothing else.

He had reached the house. There was no light in the window. Quietly he opened the door and saw the old woman on her chair, the light from the fire wavering across her face and hands. Her cheeks were scooped with shadow, her eyes glistening, her head inclined on her left shoulder. Her lips mumbled, and he saw the smooth glint of beads hanging from her hand. Standing within the door he watched her, her deep withdrawal from everything, her mind on another world. For a moment he had pity on her: she was planning and preparing, snatching a few quiet minutes in which to turn to God. Eileen's words assailed his mind again, and to dispel them he shut the door noisily. The old woman startled and gathered up her beads.

'Where's my mother?' he asked.

She pointed to the ceiling with her finger and then cleared her throat: 'The child was crying and she went up to lie beside him on top of the bed.'

He hung his cap on the knob of the banisters: 'It doesn't look as if we're going to have any tea the night. Is Mary not in? I suppose she's away stitching clothes for the Black Babies when she should be at home making a fellow his tea.' He pulled down the blind and lit the gas. The lark chirped. The old woman rubbed her eyes and blinked at the tired fire, tawdry now under the yellow gaslight.

'Sit down, Hugh, and I'll wet you a drop. Your mother's a bit jaded.'

He didn't answer her. He lay on the sofa with his arms under his head, gazing at the red walls of the kitchen and the brown banisters merging into the dark well of the stairs. The old woman passed in and out of her room carrying to the table cheese and cake which she had stored in one of her trunks.

'I suppose you like it strong?' she said as the flurry of steam whistled from the kettle.

'Anyway at all, Granny. I'm not particular.'

'It'll be well for the girl gets you — she'll have an easy handful.'

He looked at her thoughtfully and wondered had his mother told her about Eileen — it wouldn't matter even if she had. He sat at the table with his back to her and noticed how clean everything was: the fresh newspaper on the table, the wedge of cheese, and the currant cake.

'Have you kept nothing for yourself?' he said.

'To-morrow's Ash Wednesday — Lent begins and I'll have no call for them for many weeks to come.'

Until now he hadn't thought of Lent. To-night he would have to bring Eileen to the pictures; it would be the last until Easter Monday, for since he had started walking out with her some two years ago they had gone off pictures for Lent and he had gone off cigarettes.

While he was taking the tea Mary came in. Her pale face was slightly flushed, her eyes red.

'Hello, Granny! Hello, Hugh!' she greeted cheerily and kept twirling her black felt hat on her hand. 'Is there any more tea in the pot?' and without waiting for an answer she had gone over and lifted the lid. 'Will I fill your cup up for you? What about you, Granny, would you want a wee drop?'

'Mary, daughter, I'm tired drinking tea. I seem to do nothing else since I left the country.'

'You're doing well for yourself, Hugh. Cheese

and cake and plenty of butter. Is this part of Eileen's home-welcome?'

He signalled with his thumb towards the old woman.

'Och, Granny,' said Mary with mild reproach. 'It's a shame for us to be ating you out of house and home.'

'Lent's to-morrow, daughter,' and she joined her hands on her lap and began to tell them about the black fasts the people had to thole forty years ago: 'There's nothing like them fasts now! Nothing! And divil a bit of harm it done the old people. It put back bone into them and made them as tough as a thorn tree. I'm beginning to think the people nowadays are getting soft in the flesh and hard in the heart. They deny themselves nothing. They're not even civil to you in the street. I'm telling you the world's all changed and the people's all throughother.'

Hugh wasn't listening to her. He wondered would Mary lend him sixpence, but when he asked her she shook her head and whispered back to him to ask his granny. Before he had time to consider it Mary had blurted out: 'Granny, here's a fellow looking for sixpence: he wants to bring his girl to the pictures.'

He turned round: 'Don't heed her! Don't listen to her!' Already the old woman had risen, had gone into her room, and was back again with a shilling for him in her hand.

He washed quickly and went out. The kindness of the old woman trickled slowly into his mind until he found himself thinking of nothing else and trying to salve any injustice to her which he had already harboured.

Eileen was waiting for him and they walked down the street, she linking his arm.

'When you went away this evening, Hugh, I began to think. I was thinking about the old woman. Supposing she doesn't go back to the country.

99

Supposing she makes up her mind to settle down and end her days here.'

'Supposing, Eileen, the sky would fall we could catch larks. Stop this supposing! It's no use meeting trouble half-way. Of course she'll go back. From what I've heard from my mother she doesn't like the city . . . Don't be thinking about that now. It's bad making plans too far in advance,' and he laughed at quoting her own words.

Though they walked on in silence he could feel her own thoughts criss-crossing with his own and weaving in his mind a mood of doubt and weary indecision. The air was cold. Around the street lamps were haloes of colour and above the lamps darkness and the far away sky swarming with the dust of stars. Children were shouting and crying as they were put to bed. A milkman was filling the jugs reached to him from the lighted doorways, rattling the lid of his can, and sending on his horse. Eileen squeezed Hugh's arm, and he was about to say something when he saw Lena and Ann and Rita approaching them.

'Where were you wandering to this time?' he asked them.

They edged away from him in case he would clout them and Eileen smiled, opened her purse, and gave them a penny to buy sweets.

'Run on home now, your tea's ready an hour ago,' said Hugh, and when they had disappeared into the darkness Eileen looked up at him and said: 'They're great kids!'

'You'll not worry any more about the old woman?'

'I'll not, Hugh.'

'We'll go to the pictures, for to-morrow's Ash Wednesday. I'll go off cigarettes for Lent and you, Eileen, can go off worrying.'

'I'll try to!'

Chapter IX

When Mary had come into the room the old woman
was already awake and while waiting for her to dress
she lit the fire and tidied the kitchen. Getting up
before her usual hour had angered the old woman,
and Mary could hear her floundering about the room
and giving out groans of complaint. When she came
into the kitchen she did not speak, but walked to
the yard, and held out her hand as she gazed at the
cold-looking sky. There were no spits of rain — so
she could find no excuse for going back to bed. The
greyhound jumped about her feet, shook the straw
off himself and barked. She opened the back door
and he whirled out in front of her.

As she stood looking out upon the cindery waste
ground a stubborn desolation, like the clammy
wretchedness of the air, clung to her. The river was
in flood and she saw a bloated bed-tick being carried
down on the noisy water. Before her lay a broken
plate with sooty water, a mildewed boot with rusty
eye-holes; and scattered over the cinders were
cabbage leaves and sodden newspapers. She thought
of the country: the clear water in the well and the
pure wind that rushed across fields and swung the
rain-drops from the hedges. Please God, the summer
would see her back again, and in the hot days she
would sit on the big stone at the well and hear the
cool poplar leaves above her head and the larks
lacing the quivering air with song. Her conscience
would be clear too, for by that time Johnny would
surely have a job and there would be no need for
her to remain here. She told herself that she had
done the right thing in coming to the city: She had
done something she didn't like doing and surely
God would be pleased with her. During Lent she
would pray for patience.

Two old women with black shawls over their

heads and buckets in their hands passed wearily across the waste ground and paid no heed when the dog barked at them. In a weak, hoarse voice the granny called to the dog, but the old women walked on without looking to right or left, the tassels of their shawls shaking in the wind, their thin shoes sinking in the wet cart-ruts. She saw them go over to the dumps, push back the shawls from their grey heads and hoke amongst the rubbish for cinders and empty bottles. Blue smoke from burning rags rose from the dumps and fouled the air with a damp sweetish smell.

'I'm ready now, Granny,' Mary called from the scullery door. And when she came in she helped her on with her hat and coat, and presently they set off to the church.

'You're very gloomy, this morning,' Mary said, breaking a long silence.

'I'm thinking we're not as badly off as some people. I saw two old women, as old as myself, out gathering cinders, and this Ash Wednesday morning. Surely to the good God them poor women don't need to be rubbed with ashes to cleanse away their sins. Their life here is a purgatory and a cleanser. They are beginning Lent like ourselves, but there's little them people can do in the way of fast — their whole life is a lent, a fast, and a penance. I'm telling you, Mary, we'll get a quare judgment on the Last Day. There's something wrong and wicked in a world where old women are out picking cinders on an Ash Wednesday morning.'

'Don't worry about that, Granny. Sure you can do nothing and I can do nothing!' adding lightly: 'When Frankie hears that old women were out at the dumps before him he'll go wild.'

They entered the church. The choir was already chanting: 'Let us change our garments for ashes and sackcloth: let us fast and lament before the Lord: for our God is plenteous in mercy to forgive our sins.'

And when they approached the altar, Mary going first, the priest with his thumb put ashes on their heads: 'Memento, homo, quia pulvis es, et in pulverem reverteris.' Back in the seat the granny bowed her head and when she raised it she saw the people crowding back from the altar: women with shawls, women with hats, and well-dressed business men — all with their foreheads smudged with the ashes of decay. Her mind followed two old women bent over the smoking dumps, their lean fingers rooting for cinders amongst decaying rubbish; and all the time she kept telling herself that to struggle was to live and that for the poor alone every day of every year was one of fast. And as she read the gospel for the day lines of it became engraved in her mind: 'Lay not up for yourselves treasures on earth, where the rust and the moth consume, and where thieves break through and steal . . . .' And her face saddened when she thought of the bare empty grates of the cinder-gatherers and how little there was to steal from them. Life was strange; it was cruel and hard in its strangeness. She was now seventy-seven! Seventy-seven years, and though she had borne many a cross she realized that her life was smooth compared with what she had seen in the city. She sighed, and through the wet tears that were gathering in her eyes she saw the purple vestments of the priest and the gold embroidery glinting when he moved . . . Small boys kneeling beside her were leaning forward and licking the varnish off the seats, fidgeting and scratching their heads, careless and without thought. They had a long way to travel before they'd reach her age: these were their happiest days — when somebody else was working and worrying for them.

On the way home she was silent and disconsolate, and in the kitchen the children stared at the black mark on her brow and whispered: 'Granny has got ashes!' She saw Frankie closing his eyes whenever he sipped the black, sugary tea, and then his mother clouting him: 'A nice way for you to begin Lent, turning up your nose at the good tea. If you were like some people in the street you'd be going out to school this morning with a good empty belly.'

'I seen old women gathering cinders when we were getting up,' the granny put in.

'Do you hear that, Mister Frankie? They'll not leave as much cinders for you as'd fill an egg-cup . . . Get up out of your lazy bed in the morning and go over to the dumps — that'd be a good resolution to make for Lent. You usually make ones that bring you no grace.'

Frankie always resolved to give up sweets for Lent, but within a few days his pledges were broken, and except for the black tea, the fast days, and his mother making him get up for Mass in the mornings Lent for him was no different from the other seasons. This year his granny bribed him with half-pennies each time he accompanied her to the church to wait for her while she went round the Stations of the Cross. Often, when he would see the boys of the street playing football or flying long-tailed kites from the waste ground, he regretted going with her.

As he knelt in the seat he would twist with impatience, yawn, and look around him. She would stand for a long time meditating on each Station, her eyes cast sorrowfully on the mysteries of the Crucifixion. On Fridays he did the Stations with her, genuflecting and saying the prayer which she had taught him: 'We adore Thee, O Christ, and praise Thee, because by Thy cruel Passion Thou has redeemed the world.' Though the old woman's eyes were always centered on the tortured figure of Christ it was the soldiers who escorted Him that attracted Frankie's attention. At the Station 'Jesus falls the first time' the sinewy muscles of the soldiers, their thick legs, and coiling whips filled

Frankie with a terrifying awe.

'Is that cross made of wood, Granny?'

'I don't think so. I think it's a sort of delf painted brown — say your prayers like a good boy and don't be asking questions.'

She would linger, profoundly touched, at the Station 'Jesus meets the Women of Jerusalem'; and to displease her Frankie would spend the least time at that Station and hurry on to the next. On their way home she would scold him, and then talk to him of Our Lord's crucifixion and death and how it was the women who stood by Him; and she would add with bitter contempt: 'I hope you noticed there were no men — the men are selfish and hard!'

'But sure, Granny, it was Simon who helped God to carry His cross.'

'It was! But the soldiers made him do it! They'd have bate him if he had refused! They'd have battered the brains out of him. Men! It was the poor women who came out to weep for Our Saviour! It was the women's hearts that were with Him. And it was poor Veronica who wiped the precious Face!'

As Easter approached she decided to make a jersey for him and on Easter Monday they could go out to the Home together to visit Peter. The jersey was to be a surprise. But when she bought the cuts of wool and ordered him to stretch out his arms and hold each cut for her while she rolled it into a ball he got tired. He shifted from one leg to another, moved his hands up and down with a weary gesture, and contrived to unloose the wool speedily, but the wool ravelled and his Granny grew enraged when she had to pick out knots with fumbling fingers.

'That'll do you!' she shouted. 'Get out of my sight! Not another cent will you get from me!' and she took the wool from him and hung it over the back of a chair.

'You'd think it was a coil of lead I asked you to hold — You're a lazy fellow! Here I am ready to knit a jersey for you and you won't as much as help to roll the wool!

'I didn't know the wool was for me,' he answered meekly.

'Oh, the selfishness of men!' and she raised her eyes to the ceiling. 'You'll end your days on the gallows, me boyo, for not being kind to your old done granny. Mark my words! It's you should be in the Reformatory and not poor wee Peter.' The ball of wool dropped from her hands and rolled under the sofa. 'Get out of my sight before I split your skull!' and she rattled the poker and laughed when he fled through the front door. And when he was away she rebuked herself: 'Sure childer's all the same. He's not a bad wee fellow and I'm a bit too hard on him.'

On the following days it was Lena who went with her to the chapel; and when Holy Week arrived and the statues were draped with purple, the altars bare of flowers, Mary took her on the tram one evening to the Passionist Church at Ardoyne to share in the bleak wonderment of Tenebrae.

In order to get near the altar they came to the church early. A few scattered lights were lit, the statues were covered, and dark drapery hung gloomily at the back of the altar. In the purple folds of one of the statues an uncovered crozier stuck out through a slit and the old woman wondered was the statue that of St. Patrick. There was the continual shuffle of feet and the rattle of pennies on the collection plate at the porch as the people poured into the church.

On a triangular stand fourteen brown candles were lighted and on the topmost corner was a white candle burning more brightly than the rest. Presently the choir throbbed out their psalms of lamentations and all the lights in the church were extinguished except the burning candles. The old woman eyed the tiny wavering flames, for at home in her country chapel they never had a service like this. Over her head chanted the voices of the choir filling the bleak air with black desolation; and as the candles were being extinguished one by one a coldness crawled over her and she thought of death, of clay, and of corruption. She moved closer to Mary and heard her sigh: 'The apostles are falling asleep.'

A cold silence leaned over the church. A watch ticked loudly in a man's pocket and at the back of the church a child cried. The old woman recalled the weeping women of Jerusalem and wished in her heart of hearts that the apostles had been other than men. Smoke twirled up from the snuffed candles and faded into the shadows that looped from the ceiling. Gradually all the candles except the white one were dead. Tears flickered on her eyes, and when the white one was taken away for a while the chilliness of the grave fell upon her and she could hear the ponderous thumping of her own heart. Christ was dead! And in the crowded darkness of the church she realized how often she had deserted Him — following her own selfish easy ways. She wasn't long for this world and she would try now to live for Him, for others, and not for herself. She resolved to remain in the city until Johnny would no longer require her help. The resolution lightened the heaviness that was bruising her heart. She raised her head. The white candle, brighter now because of the darkness, was brought back again and placed on the apex of the triangle, and the people watching it thought of the coming Resurrection.

From the dim church they moved out, subdued and quiet, their eyes wet with tears, their faces stiff with grief. Mary took the old woman's arm and helped her down the steep steps that led to the street and to the tram. They didn't speak to one another until they reached the tram-stop.

'It's cold, Granny,' said Mary.

'It is, child!'

But each knew what the other's thoughts were: the coldness of the night did not matter — away back, in a thick gloom, the wicks of candles were hardening, the church emptying, the air warmed a little from the breaths of the congregation.

When they got back to the house Johnny was sitting with his feet on the fender and Jackie McCloskey was yarning to him, and the kitchen was filled with tobacco smoke.

'Don't stir now, Jackie,' Johnny said when the old woman and Mary came in, Mary helping her off with her hat.

'Don't let me chase you,' said the old woman.

Jackie made to rise: 'It's late and Liza will be wondering what's keeping me.'

'She's glad to get rid of you for an hour or two,' replied Johnny. 'Sure if she wanted you she'd thump the wall.' He moved his chair from the front of the fire: 'Well, what'd you think of Ardoyne to-night?'

'It was lovely, Johnny. I never seen anything as sad in all my life.'

'It's a grand church, Mrs. Griffin. And there's some fine wee men amongst them Passionists,' said Jackie.

Mary busied herself about the scullery, taking cups from their hooks and quietly arranging them on the table.

'Do you know, Jackie, what I'm going to tell you?' observed Johnny, taking the pipe from his mouth and spitting into the fire. 'There's nothing to bate the men out of the Orders. They lead a hard life — one year they could be head lad in the Order and the next year they're as equal as the newly ordained. Look at them humble wee men we have up in Ardoyne and Clonard. I don't know what it is, but some of them seculars get too bossy after a time. Man alive, Jackie, some of them wouldn't take a word from me nor you.'

'Why is it you pick out the ones with faults?' Mary cut in, as she waited for the kettle to boil. 'Why do you always forget the other ones — the simple kind men who treat us all alike? Where'd you get a better man than our own Father Teelan? — He never passes the door anytime he's in the district. There's plenty of good men amongst the seculars — men that'd give you the shoes off their feet.'

' 'Tisn't that I'm referring to at all, for I have wee seculars in my head as unworldly as St. Francis. It's their attitude to the likes of me and Jackie that I'm faulting them with. There's your granny there who knew Father Lawson when he was curate in the country. He's dead now, God be good to him. He was a poor man, but — but if you turned a word on him he went up in smoke.' He began to laugh and took the pipe from his mouth. 'Man, I'll never forget the day I doubted a decision of his when we were running the parish sports. I done it quietly, but Father Lawson turned on me and the way his jaw quivered I thought he'd take a stroke. He gripped his stick and drew himself up like a poker: "Look here, Johnny," says he. "I'm a much older man than you and if you're not satisfied with my ruling here, clear out of the field ... I'll not tolerate any insubordination!"

"Aw," says I, seeing the state he was in, "I'm sorry, Father Lawson." And I stretched out my paw to shake his. But he turned on his heel and it was only when he had simmered down that he shook my hand. But would you believe it, Jackie, he hardly ever spoke to me? Man, alive, if he had come in the next day when he was passing and said: "It's a fine day, Johnny" — just as if nothing had happened — I'd have forgot all about the whole damned business. But he didn't do it — he just went bouncing past the house like an insulted schoolboy. There's

109

bigness of mind for you!'

'In-sub-ord-in-ation!' repeated Jackie, though he didn't know the meaning of the word. 'Insubordination! A terrible word, Johnny, for a priest to use. A severe word!'

'Father Lawson was a saintly man,' the old woman said sleepily, burying herself in the arm-chair.

'Devil the row I ever had with any of them, Mrs. Griffin,' Jackie addressed her, taking out his big watch and holding it to his ear. 'I just hop in and out to them Clonard men. Some of them's the dickens on the pledge, but I always shun them sort. And do you know, I was caught not long ago: One of them asked me to take the pledge for life. He was a young man with little sense in his head and I nearly went paralysed when he popped the question.'

'And what'd you say to him?' asked Johnny.

' "Father," says I, "my wife, Liza, doesn't allow me to take the pledge." '

' "You're wife doesn't allow you?" '

' "Yes, Father, she doesn't." For she says when I'm off the beer I'm crosser than twenty she-devils out of the depths of hell and nobody could live with me.'

' "All right so," said the young priest. "But like a decent man you'll not take too much." '

' "I'll do that, Father," said I, and out I stepped as proud as a gamecock.'

'Will you sit over and take a mouthful of tea and leave the clergy to the Almighty?' said Mary. 'Sure they're human like the rest of us.'

She brought the granny her tea to the hob and fetched her slippers from the room, and before putting them on, the old woman held up her cold feet to the warm grate. While the men ate and talked she gazed dreamily into the fire, thinking of the deep comfort which enwrapped her and thinking of women, her own age, out from the early hours of the morning poking for cinders amongst the decomposing rubbish of the dumps.

Suddenly Liza thumped the wall and the old woman jumped: 'What in the name of God is that? It put the heart out of me.'

'That's Jackie's commander-in-chief giving the order to march,' laughed Johnny.

Jackie got to his feet: 'I must go before she lets another blarge out of her. It makes life easier to let the women have their own way.'

Johnny shook his head with pretended disdain: 'When a man's got no children of his own his wife makes a child out of him.'

Echoing through the thin wall they heard Liza's voice — a distorted jabbering — snapping at him: 'You always over-stay your time . . . poor people want to get to bed . . . that pipe would give the old woman jaundice . . . .'

The old woman had relapsed deeply into her arm-chair, her head drooped on her shoulder, her sunken eyes without a flicker of recognition.

'She's done to the world,' whispered Johnny. 'The journey to Ardoyne was too much for her. Help her into bed, Mary, and I'll go out for a mouthful of fresh air.'

When she had her safely in bed she sat at the fire and combed her long black hair. She sat leaning forward, her back straight, her two hands clasped round her knees, her hair shining in the gaslight. Occasionally she would tap her teeth with the comb, wondering if the coming summer would find her in the convent. She sighed contentedly. Then the old woman called out to her, and asked her to put up the window a little more, told her to look under the bed to see if the cat had got in, and finally persuaded her that there was a mouse behind one of the American trunks. To placate her she dragged out the trunks. The old woman pulled the blankets over her head and from her covered security grumbled out a warning: 'Keep your mouth

111

closed or one of them rascals would jump down your throat.'

'No, there's not a thing there only a big spider.'

'Maybe it's in my ear the noise is. But I was sure it was the scrabble of a mouse I heard.'

'Content yourself. No mouse would come into a house where there's a cat.'

'You're right, daughter, sure I should have known. Is your mother in bed, child?' she added wearily.

Hugh came in, hung his cap on the knob of the banisters, and rubbed his hands together. A lock of his black hair hung down over his brow and he flung it back with his fingers. His black eyes were shining, and he moved about with a great flourish of his shoulders.

'Good news, Mary. I'm getting a start in the brick yard after Easter. One of Eileen's sisters got in touch with the gaffer and she put in a good word for me.'

'The pit work will be the end of you,' she said coldly. 'Digging with a pick in the open, wet to the skin in the rain, won't suit you.'

'It's not in the pit I'll be working. It's in the drying-sheds.'

'One's as bad as the other. The work's too hard and it'll get you down.'

'Did the work in the jail get me down?' he said irritably.

'Speak quietly,' and she nodded her head towards the room. She took a stocking from the line that stretched across the fireplace, pushed her hand down to the heel, and stuck her finger through a hole. She commenced to darn, looking up now and again and reprimanding him for eating noisily. He said nothing, and when he sat at the fire she reproached him vexatiously for putting his dirty feet on the clean fender.

The old woman hammered the floor. Mary went in to her and was told to take the hair-brush from below the window for there was a wicked draught

112

flustering the curtains.

'I don't know how you've the patience with that woman,' Hugh said, after she had closed the room door. 'When I get this job she can go back to the country anytime she likes.'

'And how long will your job last! You'll be in for a week or two and then you'll be told there's no building being done. There's nothing secure now — nothing!'

It was useless talking to her; she was in a twisted mood. He opened an old magazine, but was too excited to read and he closed it and thought of the future. Going to the back he stood at the door and looked across the river at the brick yard. The moon shone full in his face. Black smoke from the tall chimney sullied the blue of the sky; the tarred roofs shone wetly, and here and there stacks of bricks threw shadows amongst the gleaming cart-ruts. An engine throbbed slowly like a heart-pulse, and beyond it came the snort of the suction pump draining up the grudging water from the pit. From the goat's shed sharp corners of darkness leaned on the ground. The wire of a clothes-line shone like glass, and in the jabbling water of the river shavings of light twirled and flickered before vanishing into the shadows of the banks.

He breathed in the night-air and closed the door. The shining ivy around the window rustled in the frail breeze, and sunk in the top pane was the pure reflection of the moon.

Chapter X

The warm sun shone through the window, and the lark splashed its head and wings in the water, shook itself and sent a fine spray on to the kitchen tiles. He burst into song. The old woman was dozing on

113

her chair, and to prevent the sun from putting out
the fire she had pinned a newspaper across the
bottom of the window. A smoky sunbeam was now
shining through the top pane, glittering on the
drinking-vessel in the cage and scribbling a reflection
on the ceiling. Gradually the sun stretched across
the floor to the old woman's feet; and there could
be seen her thick black stockings and her shoes slit
from the tongues to the toe-caps. The white cat lay
on its back, tearing at her stockings, and playing
with the dangling cords which did service for laces.
When the claws would touch her skin she would
push the cat gently with her toe and half open her
eyes. But the lark's song exasperated her and she
gripped the smooth handles of the chair and rocked
herself to and fro. She looked at the clock and saw
that she had been dozing for only ten minutes. The
kitchen was very warm and the lark's song seemed
to break in a thousand pieces as it re-echoed from
the walls.

'Quiet!' she shouted at it. 'Quiet there!' and she
watched his throat throbbing. She blinked her eyes
and tried to sleep again; and as the lark's warbling
echoed in her head she thought of her spring-well,
the icy water twirling up from the stony bottom,
the cool shadows of the bushes stretching over it
like wings, and out on the grass the shadows of
the poplar leaves dancing like little slippers. She
shrugged her shoulders happily. The lark continued
in a wild frenzy, his song fading in her mind to a
thin streak of sound, fading and fading till it was
only a speck, and then returning rapidly it seemed
to swell and burst in her head in whirling fragments
of splintery sound. She woke with a start, rubbed
her eyes with her forefingers, and looked at the fire.
The smoky sunbeam was now shining on the door
of her room, revealing blisters on the yellow paint
and smudges encircling the brass knob.

She got to her feet and unpinned the paper from

the lower pane. Outside, children were clapping and shouting, and she went to the door to watch them. On the sunny side of the street a group of girls was standing at a window-sill, their noisy excited chatter starting a dog to bark. Ann and Rita were there, and Lena had Oliver in his go-car and he was chewing his leather strap and shaking his bare legs. They were preparing a Queen o' May.

'I'll be the Queen!' some were shouting.

'No, let Ann Griffin be the Queen . . . she has the blackest hair.'

'I'm not going to play, Lena Griffin, if you don't make me the Queen,' huffed a little girl who had a silver-painted cardboard crown. 'And I'll go home with my crown too.'

After much disputing, arranging, crying, and hand-clapping they decided that the girl who owned the crown should be the Queen and Ann Griffin, because of her black fringe and black eyes, should be the Darky. Lena brought Ann into the house, pushing past the granny who leaned against the jamb.

'Oh, you pair of tom-boys!' she cried, when Lena emerged again. Ann had her face blackened, a bowler hat on her head, and a pair of Frankie's trousers tied to her waist.

Presently the Queen was crowned at a window-sill: a green paper apron was pinned on to her, a veil, the remnants of a window curtain adorned her head, and yellow crepe paper was fastened to her wrists and ankles. The group of girls formed up in twos; in front of the procession were the Queen and the Darky, the two biggest girls escorting them, one holding a yard-brush and the other a tin-box with a slit made in it for money. In high-pitched voices they began to sing:

> 'The Darky said he'd marry her,
>   Marry her,
>   Marry her,

115

The Darky said he'd marry her,
Because she is the Queen.'

and off they danced down the street, the Queen's
paper apron rising and falling, her veil streaming
behind her. The granny halted them and put a
penny in the box.

At the bottom of the street they met a rival
Queen and with shrill cries they hurled insults at
one another: 'Your crown's made of pasteboard . . .
Yous have no crown and yiz are all jealous . . . Your
oul' Queen needs her face washed . . . Ha, ha, look
at the paper apron and the yellow paper to hide her
dirty heels . . . .'

Lena with stiff, exaggerated dignity marshalled
her clan, and standing in front of the Queen, the
yard brush held aloft, marched arrogantly forward;
then with the mechanical flourish of a drum-major
she lowered the brush, stretched it horizontally in
front of the Queen and with a haughty voice gave
the order to sing. With victorious glee her followers
chorused:

'Our Queen can tumble on her head,
Tumble on her head,
Tumble on her head,
Our Queen can tumble on her head . . .'

And the Queen would grip the horizontal pole and,
with flying trousseau, would vault over it to the
cheers of her retinue and the silent jealousy of her
rival. Up and down the street they skipped, the
Darky holding up her trousers, the Queen tumbling,
the tin-box rattling, and babies being ushered up in
wooden carts with buckled pram-wheels. The
procession disappeared round the top corner and a
great stillness came over the warm street. Upstair
windows were flung open and a white jug or a brass
bed-rail could be seen in the dark interior. The sun

116

shone full on the old woman's face and threw her shadow into the small porch behind her. She felt the hot sun oozing through her hands, and she thought of her field in the country where Johnny had gone to put in a few drills of potatoes for her. The leaves would be thickening on the hedges now, the roads drying, and her hens beginning to lay. She sighed heavily and walked through the kitchen to the waste ground.

She stood on the river bank, looking down at the dry-topped stones and the glittering bubbles sailing under the red arch. The air was warm and every noise was intensified in the quivering heat: carts tippled their loads at the dumps with a crash as loud as thunder, the unloosed horses jangled their chains and stamped nervously. Fish-tails of light rippled up from the river and made her eyes blink. She shaded her eyes as she gazed beyond the brick yard to the fresh green fields which sloped towards the mountain. With her hands in her sleeves she walked slowly up and down, feeling the cinders crunch under the thin soles of her shoes. She was opposite the dumps now, but the sweetish smoke that came from its damp fires almost sickened her. She turned and saw an old man enjoying the sunshine; a woman linked him, her eyes fixed on the unsteady movement of his shuffling feet.

'Now who would that be?' she asked herself, and with strained anxiety saw the woman help him towards a chair. The old man sat down, his overcoat around him, his trembling hands on his knees, the colour of death on his face. The woman came out of the yard with a glass of water in her hand and held it to his lips.

'That poor man's far through! It's the last sun he'll feel,' the granny said to herself, as she made for home, moistening her dry lips.

When she came in she stood on a chair and reached for the black bottle which she had placed in a dark

117

corner of the scullery. Since the warm days had set in she had made for herself a mixture with brown sugar and treacle and, for at least a week, she would leave it on the top shelf in the scullery. 'Her medicine!' she called it, and on hot days she would pour some into a mug, retire to the cool seclusion of her room and there, sitting on the low bed, she would sip it languidly, sifting out its shallow flavour with many smacks of her lips and quizzical expressions from her eyes. To-day she made a wry face as she took the first sip: 'Aw, be the holy, I'm poisoned! It's as flat as rainwater'. and she smelt the bottle: 'I'm afraid that Hugh fella has helped himself and filled it up with water.' She held the bottle up to the light and measured the height of the liquid. She smiled cunningly, hammered on the cork with the palm of her hand, and with her thumb-nail scratched the height on the label. She got up angrily on the chair again, but as she stretched to the top shelf the chair tilted. There was a stumble and then she crashed heavily to the floor, the bottle breaking in bits in the jar-tub. A sharp pain seared through her left arm and speckles of light shimmered before her eyes. For a while she lay still, afraid to move. Her left wrist began to swell. Her heart fluttered wildly. She tried to rise, but she had no strength. The noise had frightened the lark, and from where she lay she saw him flitting from perch to perch and clawing at the bars with outstretched wings. He chirped plaintively.

Outside she could hear the children's voices rising in song as they came down the street. Surely Lena would be in for something; they were always running in and out when you didn't want them. The singing became louder and she saw their heads bobbing past the window, the shining silver crown, and Ann's bowler hat . . .

'The Darky said he'd marry her . . . marry her . . . marry her.' They had passed. Everything was still

118

again. She could smell the treacle and sugar that had spilt in the sink and could feel the coldness of the tiles creeping into her bones. Oh, why in God's name didn't someone come! A blue-bottle sailed in through the scullery window, buzzed angrily against the pane and then flew down to the sink, and she knew by his quiet manoeuvres that he was gorging himself in 'her medicine'. Back again came the children and halted outside the kitchen window. She tried to call to Lena, but her weak, strange voice was smothered in the ceaseless babble of the excited children. Then without warning they all scattered like a flock of pigeons. There's no sense in children's heads at all; running like mad people up and down, down and up. She would get her death if no one came in soon; and she thought of the old man out in the sun and the corpse-colour of his face.

'Liza! . . . Mrs. McCloskey! . . . Mrs. McCloskey!' she called in a whimpering voice; if only she could crawl into the kitchen and give the wall a few thumps. She tried to move, but streaks of pain combed through every joint. 'I'm at death's door now,' she complained. 'And nobody cares!'

Slowly the sun came round and shone into the scullery, and lay on her finger-nails and on her swollen wrist. A clock chimed four. God in Heaven, nobody might come in till five! Where was Frankie? — playing football, I suppose. And Mary? —down stitching with the nuns. And them senseless children with their Queen o' May and poor wee Oliver starving with hunger! Poor Peter — if he were here he'd be in helping his granny! This is my punishment for accusing Hugh — I'm sure he never touched the bottle. It's all gone now — the whole thing; every blessed drop gone down the sink.

Her left arm throbbed, and she shut her eyes as the spasm of pain weakened her. Gently she put her brow on the tiles and felt their coldness burning her forehead. She heard McCormick's clutch of children, yelling and fighting, and heard the father stampeding out to the yard to smack them. Then she heard him chopping sticks and whistling to himself.

'Mister McCormick!' she raised her voice. But he continued to whistle, to break his sticks, and to hammer out the bent nails on the tiles. That wee stupid man would hear nothing! And them fish-boxes that he buys gather all the cats in the neighbourhood — a body can't get asleep at night!

A cracked tile with dirt in its corner annoyed her, and she closed her eyes and surrendered herself to uncontrollable misery. All at once there was a sound of laughter, and on looking up she saw Mary, hat in hand, standing outside the kitchen window, her black hair shining in the sun.

'Mary! . . . Mary!' she screeched, and her head fell limply forward, and she felt herself sinking into her spring-well and the water receding from her as she fell. Blurred voices came and went, stretching thin, then broad, like being inside a focusing telescope.

'Are you all right, Granny?' Mary was asking, as she sprinkled her with holy water.

Liza McCloskey hurried out to her house and rushed back with a bottle in her hand.

'Here's a thimbleful of whiskey. Get me a spoon, quick!'

'Will I get the doctor and the priest, Liza?'

'Wait, child, till we get her into bed first. She mightn't be too bad.'

While they were putting her to bed Kate came in, a full basket in her hand, after tramping the soles off her shoes to buy things cheap.

'I knew something would happen that old woman! I knew it! . . . Where were you, Mary? . . . Where was Lena? . . . I can't be two places at once,' and she hung up her hat and coat and tied on an apron.

'We'll have to get the doctor — more expense.

And Johnny away in the country. How did it happen?' she rhymed like a litany. 'But we needn't complain. It's a blessing of God's it didn't happen in the country . . . That's what I've always been saying to Johnny . . . Didn't happen in the country.'

She stood at the bedside feeling the hot sweaty forehead and looking with a pained expression at the blue swollen wrist. 'Are your legs all right?' she asked. The old woman opened her eyes and nodded.

Liza went for the doctor, and when his car drove up Mary went to the window and saw the children scrambling around the door and the neighbours gathering in groups. The doctor was a young man, fat of face, black haired, and a moustache like a smear of boot-polish. Would he be capable? she asked herself. How long it took him to get out of the car, and stopping too to pat the children on the head. And there he was going over to talk to that old gossiper — it's a wonder he would be bothered with her. She opened the door and stared across the street at him. He came over slowly, carrying an attache case, and passed into the room with a bland smile. In a few minutes he was out again, standing on the kitchen floor smoking a cigarette.

'Is she bad, Doctor?' Mary asked, rubbing her hands.

'Not too bad: a fractured wrist which will take a long time to heal in a woman of her age. She suffers slightly from shock and you'll have to keep her warm and give her plenty of hot drinks . . . Would you happen to have two boards that would do me for splints?'

Mary went out and knocked at McCormick's back door. 'Stick' opened at her knock, a hatchet in his hand, chips of wood on his hair and clothes. She looked down at his diminutive figure:

'Stick . . . Eddie,' she corrected herself quickly. 'My granny fell and broke her wrist and the doctor's in with her and he wants two splints.'

'Come in, come in, till I have a look,' and he closed the door behind her. 'That's too bad about the old woman. Josephine will be sorry to hear about it — she's out at her Baby Club.'

Chopped sticks were strewn about the yard; in a corner lay a heap of rusted nails; and the warm air was heavy with the sweet smell of wood. Three dirty-faced children smiled out at her from the bare window in the scullery. In a minute Stick was out with boards of different lengths:

'Here's boards as light as a feather. I got them in a clothier's rubbish heap. Tell the doctor to take what he likes and if they're too long I'll soon shorten them.'

As he opened the door to let her out a little bare-footed boy tried to dodge out along with her, but his father gripped him by the jersey and pulled him back.

'Eating again,' he said to him. 'Mary, don't ever get married — children would break your heart. I can't manage them without Josephine.' And as she left she heard a child crying and Stick yelling at them: 'You've disgraced me before the decent neighbours! Disgraced me! Whinging for bread and yous only after yer good dinners.' But in a minute she knew he would be whistling, tying his sticks in bundles, and straightening out the bent nails.

Lena, Ann, and Rita sat quietly on the sofa, speaking in whispers, and watching their mother and Mary moving in and out of the wee room. When Hugh came in from his work in the brick yard the children were already in bed and the kitchen was cool and quiet after the heat of the day. Brick dust bronzed his arms and sweaty face. He closed the scullery door and took off his working trousers and heavy boots. He filled the jar-tub with water and stripped to the waist. The heat of the day had exhausted him, and as he plunged his brown arms into the cold water and soused his face and neck he

122

felt with a pang of relief the refreshing coldness anoint his tired limbs. He pulled on a shirt and came into the kitchen. He felt cool. The dust was still engrimed about his eyelashes, making his eyes look very bright. As he waited for his tea he put his arms on the table and rested his head on them.

'You didn't hear about your granny?' Kate asked as she toasted bread for him at the bars of the grate.

'No, has she gone home?' he mumbled without enthusiasm.

'Gone home! What put that in your head? She has broken her wrist and she'll be in bed for some weeks . . . She's asleep now.'

He raised his head, combed back his black hair with his fingers, but didn't speak. As he bent his head down to his cup Mary corrected him and told him not to eat like an animal.

'Look here, madame!' he eyed her. 'I'm tired listening to you. When I come in tired and sore after a hard day's work I should get peace to take my tea. Your manners may be all right for a convent, but they don't suit a brick yard labourer.'

'That'll do, Hugh,' his mother admonished. 'You needn't take a correction so ill.'

'I'm tired listening to her!'

'And, Mother,' Mary continued, 'he's callous. There's that old, done woman in there and he never as much as said he was sorry to hear about her broken wrist.'

He buttered a piece of bread recklessly and let the knife fall on to the floor.

'Hugh, son, take your tea. She doesn't mean a word of it. Sure everyone knows you're as sorry as the rest of us. Don't heed her, Hugh, she's overwrought.'

'I'm not one that makes an exhibition of my grief — I feel it all the same.'

'I'm sure you do!' Mary added sarcastically.

'Now, in God's name, that will do! Arguing and

fighting like this, comes to no good! I don't want
to hear another word from any of you.'

Mary went into the scullery and pretended to
work around the sink. The remark about the convent had hurt her; in future she would not interfere
with him — Eileen can teach him his manners when
she marries him. She came into the kitchen, lifted
the tea-pot from the hob, and filled up his cup for
him. He went on eating and took no notice of her.
She relapsed into silence, went quietly into the
wee room, and stood at the window gazing into
the bare, cheerless yard.

Chapter XI

That night the old woman was restless, and when a
spasm of pain ransacked her arm she tried to
smother the moans that involuntarily crushed out
from between her lips. A clammy, nervous sweat
soaked her forehead and trickled into the loose
folds of her neck. Her arm in its sling rested on
the quilt, and as the night grew old she tried to
move into a more comfortable position, but darts of
pain jagged through her smashed wrist, and she
closed her eyes with the weariness of complete
resignation. In the deep silence of the night she
listened to the quick pound of her heart and to the
loud tick-tock from the clock in the kitchen. Once
she dozed over and then wakened with a start, her
eyes wide open with fright. A moon had risen and
was shining high in the window. The ivy leaves
patterned the floor.

She turned her head. On the table was a glass of
water, the moonlight shining through it and glinting
on a spoon. She licked her dry, hard lips and
swallowed with difficulty. She turned her head from
the table, but the glass of water had sealed itself
in her mind, consuming her with a fierce thirst. Her

lips and throat were as dry as paper. If she moved to the edge of the bed she might be able to stretch out and reach the glass; she tried to rise, but the tearing pain of her arm weakened her and she lay back exhausted.

Then the clock in the kitchen began to strike and since she had no strength of will to control her wayward mind from counting the slow strokes her head seemed to sway with a pendulous motion. Soon the neighbouring clocks would begin their chime, and while she waited, knowing how their sinister inconsistency would taunt her, her whole body quivered in a confused jangle of pain.

'Kate! Mary!' she called hysterically, and sweat dribbled down her back. 'Mary!' she cried, in a voice that trailed to a whisper.

There was the sound of someone moving upstairs; the banisters creaked, and then Mary padded into the room, a coat over her nightdress, a candle in her hand.

'Did you call, Granny?' she asked, and in the candlelight saw the dark rings round the eyes and the sweat glistening on her forehead.

'Granny, did you call?' and she bathed her forehead with a damp cloth and filled up the glass with fresh, cold water. The old woman opened her eyes and smiled wanly. In the yard the dog gave a muffled bark.

'It was them clocks ... waiting for them to strike ... a weakness came over me.'

'Take a wee sip of the cold water — it'll do you good,' and she put an arm under her head and held the glass to her lips.

'Thank God,' she breathed with relief, and added after a pause, 'Mary, don't leave me ... Sleep at the foot of the bed ... I'm done!'

'Nonsense, Granny. The doctor says you'd mend in a few weeks.'

'Och, child, what does that doctor know? — He's

too young for the likes of me. I'm done, God take care of me! And if anything happens, Mary, I'm to be buried in the country. Johnny knows the spot. He'll do things decent. Get me a yellow coffin — not one of them horrible, black things. My twopence-a-week insurance will cover all.'

'Oh, what a way to be talking,' said Mary, applying a damp cloth to the hot forehead. 'Don't be fretting. You'll be home again — never fear. Close your eyes now and I'll lie at the foot of the bed. Don't be worrying. With God's help you'll soon be all right,' and she patted her on the shoulder and stroked the grey head.

But stabled securely in the old woman's mind was the thought of death and she did not permit Mary to banish it from her.

'I'll never set foot nor eye on my own home again,' and her mouth quivered as the words fell from it. 'There's a long journey afore me. I'll be going home, but it'll be . . . in . . . a . . .' her voice broke and she sobbed like a child.

'There, there,' Mary said gently, as if she were placating little Oliver. She bit her lip to keep from crying. Her voice trembled, and turning round to the table she blew out the candle.

'You've been all kind to me,' the old woman went on, her thoughts following a track of their own. 'Everyone of you was good to me. I'm not complaining. Johnny was a good, good son — poor man he wrought hard in his day; he was always misfortunate. I'd do anything for Johnny — any mortal thing. He'll give me a nice funeral. It's all I ask now. And you'll remember me in your prayers.' She pulled out a handkerchief from under the pillow and her rosary rattled. 'I thought I'd be back by the summer. But I'm done, Mary. I'll never get over this.'

Mary lay quiet, her mind jumbled with indecision: wondering if she should go for Father Teelan, and wondering again if the thoughts of death came from an overwrought mind. It was after three. The moon-light lay thick on the walls and the ivy leaves stirred faintly. She would wait until daybreak and maybe go for Father Teelan then. But while she turned the idea over and over in her mind she slipped into an unsettled slumber.

The bright light from the May morning awoke her, and she lay still and heard the dog's paws on the yard-tiles and the first tram moving quickly to the heart of the city. She rubbed her eyes, which were usually inflamed after a night's hemstitching, and looked up at the old woman. Her face was shrunken with pallor, the hair greyer than she had ever seen it, the sunken lips colourless. The purple finger-nails of her broken wrist hung lifelessly between the swathes of cotton wool. Quietly she lay back and waited for her to waken.

The uprising sun strengthened and the lace curtain threw a reflection like water on the ceiling. With her hands under her head she lay gazing round the room. She noticed a match-strike on the blue wall and a crack on the glass which domed the statue of St. Anthony. She recalled the wet wintry day she had helped Hugh to move the bed and to tidy the room for the granny's arrival. God knows it was an unfortunate change for one so old! She looked at the fireplace which she had black-lacquered, the crucifix she had nailed to the wall, and the cake of scented soap lying on the saucer beside the pink jug. The soap was thin now and cracked, and the room seemed smaller, cluttered as it was with two American trunks, clothes hanging from a dozen nails in the door, and the bed so low that she felt she was sleeping on the floor.

The old woman stirred, sighed deeply, and blinked at the sunlight skimming the yard-wall.

'How do you feel this morning, Granny?'

'Bravely, daughter, bravely,' she answered huskily.

'Would you take a drop of tea if I made it?'

'It would be welcome — my throat's like sand-paper. Would you raise me a wee bit on the pillows? — I must have slipped during the night.'

Very carefully she propped the pillows under her shoulder and pushed down the window to let in more air. Then she heard the window-blind in the kitchen swirl up on its roller, the ashes being raked, and the quietness fade from the house.

Kate came into the room, her head thrust forward, her sleeves rolled up. The old woman smiled weakly when Kate put a hand on her forehead.

'Thank God, you're nice and cool this morning. I'll make you a good cup of tea and toast and boil you an egg. Later on we'll get Father Teelan in to see you, and Johnny will be back from the country.'

The sun grew brighter, slanting out of the room into the yard. The water tap in the scullery gushed loudly as Hugh got ready for work, and she heard him shouting: 'Where's the stud I left on the wee table?' Then the children came crowding in to see her, the sleep vanishing from their eyes as they gazed at the sling and the blue finger-nails.

When they had gone to school Mary swept out the room, smoothed out the creases from the checked quilt and folded a towel over the pink jug. The room was tidy now — cool and fresh, and fit for any critical visitor. She washed the old woman's face, combed the grey hair, parting it down the middle and brushing it flat at each side.

'I never thought it would come to this.'

'Come to what?' asked Mary.

'That I'd be so helpless I couldn't comb my own hair or wash a handkerchief. My independence is broken!'

Mary pinned the grey shawl about her shoulders, and propped her with the pillows to a sitting posture. Her hands were outside the blankets, the free hand plucking at the loose flesh on her neck or counting her beads as she offered up her morning

128

prayers.

As the days wore on white clouds sailed past her window and she could watch the May rain glittering on the pane and drops coming together and trailing a line of light down to the sash. She grew stronger. She could listen with patience now to the lark in its cage singing in a wild frenzy and reminding her of her own field. And she looked forward to the children bringing primroses and placing them in a glass jam-jar of water beside her St. Anthony, and they in turn would smile at her, waiting for the hand to grope under the pillow and bring out the few sweets that she had hidden in a paper bag.

She got Johnny to cut down the ivy from the window and he, himself, in order to be near her, commenced to dig up part of the waste ground around his goat's shed and make a plot for vegetables. Throughout that month of May he worked day and evening breaking up the hard cindery ground. Frankie carried boxes of mould from the fields, and in order to erect a fence he salvaged from the dumps old rusty pieces of tin. Stick McCormick made a rough wooden gate for him, and towards the end of the month Johnny had his plot finished. From the wooden gate a path of broken tiles and red brick ran down to the goat's shed, at each side were three ridges and in them were young cabbage plants and seedlings of lettuce, scallions, and parsley. The fence was a ramshackle of corrugated tin lashed to old bedsteads and iron staves.

As each day passed Johnny smiled contentedly as he watched the showers of rain forming at the mountain and trailing their broken fabric across the fields towards the waste ground. His seedlings grew in strength and sprouted in fresh green rows above the cindery ridges. In the evenings Jackie McCloskey would come out, pipe in mouth, and peer over the fence.

'Man, Johnny, they're thriving nicely,' and he

129

would squirt a spit beside the bed of growing lettuce. 'Liza's naggin' at me, day in, day out, to dig up a patch. I tell her it's too late in the season to be thinkin' of them things.'

'Come on in through the gate,' Johnny would say with as much ceremony as a prize gardener.

Jackie would lift the hasp, walk down the uneven path, and sit on a bench beside the goat's shed. Johnny with his sleeves rolled up, the greyhound lying at his feet, would light his pipe. They would lean their backs against the shed and Johnny would talk about the diseases of plants, about slugs, and the best way to save seed. Jackie would pinch the head off a young scallion and munch it with affected relish.

'Great medicine, Johnny,' he would say.

'Do you know what I'm going to tell you — a glass of porter and a few scallions and salt is the best sleeping draught on God's earth. Wait'll them scallions is ready and we'll celebrate some fine evening.'

'It's great health,' Jackie would answer, spitting through the gaps in the fence.

'Them McCormicks have the fence destroyed on me. They're always climbing over it looking for their ball. I told Stick about it and he said he'd skelp blazes out of them.'

'Skelp blazes out of them! Sure he lets them do whatever they damned well like. Why didn't you tell his missus — she's the girl'd fairly scatter them to their boxes.'

An old rag would blow against the fence and catch in the barbed wire. The wind would stir the fluttering pieces of paper and thread that stretched across the parsley bed, the greyhound would snap at the flies, and Jackie would sigh and cross his legs with great contentment. Sometimes with his sleeve he would polish the silver medal and chain that stretched across his waistcoat. The medal had been awarded for a swimming championship, but Jackie had bought it in a pawnshop and wore it proudly on his watch-chain. When anyone read the medal's inscription and said: 'You must be a great swimmer, Jackie,' Jackie would answer quietly: 'That was in my young days. I'm a bit stiff now.'

Johnny would watch with an ironical smile how carefully he blew his breath on the medal and polished it with his sleeve. He would spit on the ground, stamp his foot on it, and say: 'Some day the two of us will go to Lough Neagh and have a good swim to ourselves.'

'Ai, ai,' Jackie would answer abstractedly, and he would raise his head and look towards the back of the house where a veiny pattern on the red brick showed where the ivy had been cut down.

'The old woman's on the mend?' he would ask, ignoring the reference to swimming.

'She is, but she's still in the splints.'

As they talked Liza usually passed on her way to see the old woman and looking over the fence at the two men she would shout in a bantering tone: That's the way, Johnny; teach that lazy man of mine how to grow a spud,' and with a twist of her head she would pass through the Griffins' yard and into the wee room. There she would sit on a chair gossiping to the old woman as she lay propped on the pillows. They would talk for an hour or two, Liza telling the old woman how she had met Jackie at the jumble sale when they were both bidding for the same pair of delf dogs. They would exchange pinches of snuff and the old woman in turn would tell with many sweeps of her free arm about the last time she had to lie up as helpless as any child: 'Do you know, Liza, when I was forty-six years of age I had to lie in the Ballymena hospital for six full weeks with my gall stones?'

'Tush, tush,' Liza would say, rolling her hands under her apron.

'And one of my gall stones was as big as a turkey egg. It weighed six ounces. I tell you, Liza, it was the talk of the hospital.'

'I never heard the like of that,' Liza would answer and Kate would carry in cups of tea and Liza would always read the tea-leaves. Sometimes Kate would help Oliver to walk into the room and she would lift him on to the bed where he would wheel his toy motor up and down the hills and slopes of the blankets.

In the evenings Hugh came in from work and his mother would tell him to go in and see the old woman.

'She'll not fade away till I get my tea,' he would reply sullenly.

'Go on in now. Sure she has heard you coming in.'

'I'll go when I get something to eat,' and he would close the scullery door and begin to wash.

In silence Kate would make his tea, and when he had finished he would slowly smoke a cigarette, go into the room, and stand awkwardly at the door.

'How's your wrist to-day?'

'It's on the mend, Hugh. Are you not sitting down?'

'Eileen's waiting on me,' and he would go into the kitchen, put on his cap, and go down to Eileen Curran's.

'He's a strange fellow,' the granny would say to herself and she would glance at the faded primroses and think of the kindness of the children and of Mary and Frankie and Peter. 'It's strange the different natures there is in one family.'

Sometimes when the room was quiet the white cat would find its way through the open window and lie beside her on top of the bed.

'How did that pest of blazes get in her!' Johnny shouted one evening when he had seen the quilt covered with hairs.

132

'I invited her,' his mother answered him with a fixed look. 'She's good company for an old done woman.'

Towards the end of June the splints were taken off and she got Mary to put them into one of her trunks. Mary massaged the arm with her soft fingers and soon the old woman was able to use her knitting needles, and when the children were at school Kate often heard her singing old songs to herself. But at night the woman's mind was clamorous with a grating fear. She would re-live the day she had toppled off the chair, and she would waken in a cold sweat and stretch her foot to see if Mary was still in the bed. Mary would give her a drink of cold water. She would become talkative and tell her about the country, the fine men that were in it and how a month or two in Toome would soon scatter the pallor from her cheeks.

'Did you ever think of living in the country, Mary?' she asked her one night.

'Och, I was always content to be here!'

'The country's lovely, Mary. Then there's the Bann and Church Island. You'll have to go on the pilgrimage there and see the stones where St. Patrick prayed. Did you ever see them? No! It's a sight worth seeing. His very finger marks is on the stones. Poor man, he must have prayed night, noon, and morn to wear out holes in them hard rocks.'

To all her wheedling remarks of the country Mary listened with respectful gravity and already foresaw what was uppermost in the old woman's mind. Until she was stronger she would humour her, and then some night in secret she would reveal to her that in the coming September she would enter a convent, and once there she would pray for them all and ask God to give them His grace of final perseverance.

Chapter XII

In the warm summer afternoons when the waste ground was smothered with heat Kate would take a chair through the wooden gate of the garden and place it firmly on the path, a small box beside it. The old woman would come out leaning on a stick, a black coat on her, a red flannel about her head. She would sit on the chair and place her slippered feet on the wooden box. Her snuff, her prayer beads, and a white handkerchief were always in her pocket. The sun would shine with great strength and she would push back the red flannel and feel the hot rays anoint her hair and ooze through the transparent flesh on her wrists. She would turn her hands on her lap and gaze wearily at the crinkled, shiny flesh and the delta of blue veins. Sometimes if Johnny were in the country the greyhound would follow her into the garden, put his head on her lap, lick her hands, and then lie under the bench at the goat's shed.

Through the gaps in the fence she could see the river itself, thin and shrunken, knuckled with dry stones and ribbed here and there with rusty wire; and from the dumps, as always, there arose thin smoke stretching towards the deep bowl of the sky. But when a vagrant breeze would carry the sweet, sickly smoke to the garden she would take a pinch of snuff and guard herself with her handkerchief. Specks of soot would fall on the cabbage leaves and bees would forage in the throats of the nasturtiums weighing down the heavy stems.

The soil in the lettuce bed would be parched with the sun, but under their leaves it was black and cool, holding grimly to the water which Frankie or Johnny had sprayed upon them.

Over the top of the mountain white massing clouds would slowly rise and twist, and float with majestic purity towards the sun. Their shadows

134

would scatter over the mountain, approach her across the fields, and peel the sunshine from under her feet. She would feel the cold then, and very foolishly look round to see if a door were open. Her eyes would alight on the lark's cage hanging from a nail on the yard-wall. It was pleasant to listen to him singing in the open where his voice could stretch echoless and unimpeded. But as the summer dwindled, his songs became infrequent, and he was content to give little plaintive calls or bath himself in the dish of water that was already warming in the sun. And as the old lady watched him fluffed out on his sod, memoried fragments would coalesce in her mind and bruise her heart with an unbearable longing — and she was a girl again, setting out over the bare hills to count the young lambs, passing wet-gleaming furrows in the fields, seeing rain-drops on the handles of a plough, or listening to the larks finding their voices because the spring was here. She would sigh heavily, idly lift her stick and tap it on the wooden box or prod it at the chips of delf that lay strewn on the soil.

The white clouds would break apart and the sun renew its strength, and with a rush of wings pigeons would fly overhead and sprinkle flakes of shadow on her lap. Opposite she could see the heat quivering on the tarred roofs of the brick yard, and she would think of Hugh, the dust coarsening his throat and lying in the sweaty wrinkles of his brow.

Hugh as he trundled his barrow over the iron plates that made a path in the dust, would sometimes pause to wipe the sweat from his face and gaze across the river to the sloping garden where he could see the old woman in her black coat and the scarlet flannel round her neck. He would clear his throat and spit on the red dust which choked everything about him. His shirt was always open at the neck, his sleeves bare to the elbows, his skin bronzed with sun and sweat. He would lift the smooth handles of

135

his barrow and feel the scorching heat rise thickly from the ground. But one thought controlled his mind — if the old woman would go back to the country Eileen and himself could get married and get the wee room. In the suffocating heat of the drying-shed he would place bricks, like wet slabs of chocolate, on the hot plates and see the steam rising from them and mingling with the sunshine that streamed through the fluted walls. At the door of the shed was a bucket of cold water and he would sit beside it on the shaft of his barrow and drink mug after mug of the water while around him the floor shook with the throb of engines, men shouted to one another, and in his mind his one thought grew restless.

Going home one evening, tired and cross, he met his mother at the garden gate bringing in the chair.

'I'm thinking the old woman's here too long,' he said sharply. 'She can go back to the country, for I'm earning good money and we have no call for her.'

His mother hesitated and her hands gripped the back of the chair. She looked at him and noticed the strain on his face.

'But, Hugh, son, she couldn't go back yet,' she said quietly. 'She's badly failed, the creature. Wait'll the end of the summer.'

'I'm tired waiting!'

'Waiting?' She evaded and tried to smile. 'Sure she doesn't meddle with you.'

'You know rightly, mother, what's in my mind. Hasn't Mary told you? I'm going to get married soon and I'd like the wee room.'

'Hugh, son, there's plenty of time. Sure Eileen can wait a wee while longer and we'll only be too glad to welcome her in amongst us. The doctor says the old woman is far through. There's holes in her shoulder blades you could hide an orange in.'

'I'm not wishing her dead,' he said and hitched a stone over the ground to the river.

'Sure, I know, Hugh. Sure, I know. But I'm only telling you what's in the doctor's mind.'

'And I'm only telling you what's in my mind. I'm earning good money in the brick yard and I give you nearly every penny of it.'

His mother leaned on the back of the chair and with a remote expression gazed beyond the river to the sloping fields and the mountain. The evening sun browned the far off hay rucks. She bit her lip and lifted the chair. Hugh looked at her coldly, and when the greyhound jumped around him he paid no heed to it.

In a heavy silence he took his tea and when he had finished he did not go into the wee room to speak to his grandmother. He hurried out. He had arranged to meet Eileen in the Dunville Park — a square patch of ground with high railings which islanded it from the trams and the traffic. He was early and he sat on one of the round-backed seats, his shadow lengthening in front of him. Squads of children paddled their feet in the basin of the fountain and above them the lowering sun made a rainbow with the sparkling jets of water. A group of workless men came near him and one of them tied a dog by the leash to the seat, and another took out a marble and pressed it into the ground with the heel of his boot. He made three holes, swept the dust away with his cap, and marked them with chalk rings. Hugh got up and moved towards the quiet summer house, but there he saw the floor covered with spits and two old men hunched in carven attitudes over a game of draughts. He left them to their game and sat on a vacant seat amongst shiny laurel bushes.

Eileen came in through a side gate and waved to him. He sat sideways, his legs crossed, one arm drooped over the back of the seat. She was dressed in a light grey costume, a scarlet bag under her arm, her patent shoes catching the sunlight. To embarrass her he stared at her feet, and smiled when she walked

137

ungainly. She sat beside him, her face assuming an expression of affront.

'Well?' he said.

'Well, yourself, that's a trick to play on people — staring at them like that' — she hoped that he would admire her costume, but he said nothing and she knew that something had annoyed him. 'Are you here long?'

'I've just arrived,' and he flicked a pebble into a laurel bush, and a leaf shook. 'I had a row with my mother.'

'Another one?' and she fluffed out her fair hair.

'I don't want any codding!'

She became grave and stretched out a hand to his: 'Hugh, I'm only joking. Don't worry about the row and everything will turn out all right.'

At the fountain two barefooted boys began to fight and their followers gathered round, encouraging them with shouts and pushes. Little girls wheeled their go-cars to the side and a dripping terrier ran around with a stick in his mouth. The parkranger approached and the boys scattered and shouted nicknames at him.

'Wee fellas are always fighting, Hugh.'

He combed his black hair and his fingers and lit a cigarette. The parkranger moved off, and in ones and twos the children slunk back and splashed in the fountain as if nothing had happened. Hugh moved closer to Eileen and told her about the row and how he had mentioned to his mother about marriage.

'What did she say about me?' she asked eagerly.

'She'd be glad to have you in the house — that's what she said.' He puffed at the cigarette and flicked the ash on to the cinder path. 'But I'm going to tell you this — she'll have none of us in the house if she doesn't send the old woman back to the country. We can get a room or maybe a house of our own.'

138

'We could never get a house except one of them new ones and they're too dear. Twelve and six a week they're asking for them and there's only two rooms in them and a kitchen. It's a crying out shame the way the people are frauded.

'And what do you think we could do?'

'Wait, Hugh, wait for a wee while longer and maybe things will turn out all right,' and she looked at the mother-of-pearl button on her shoe.

'Wait! Wait! — I'm tired listening to that damned word. The old woman will never go back to the country — she's not able to look after herself. And sure she might linger for God knows how long. She'd be better off in the Union where they've paid nurses to look after them.

'The Workhouse! Any place but that!' Eileen became reflective and no longer saw the playing children.

Everything that he had said was wrong! He threw the half-smoked cigarette into the laurel bush, and with his hands drooped between his knees saw it smouldering on the clay. At his feet was a piece of withered orange skin and he pushed it with his toe. He heard the men disputing over their game of marbles and saw a young mother push her pram towards the gate. Suddenly the sprays from the fountain were turned off, and the children realizing what was wrong began to boo the parkranger and scamper off for home. The two old men languidly closed their folding draught-board and as they passed Hugh he heard one say: 'If I had made that shift!' and the other mimic him contemptuously: 'If you had made that shift!'

A hand-bell was rung and Hugh and Eileen got up, went out of the park, and walked along the Springfield Road. The street lamps were lit, shining weakly because of the long twilight and the red glow in the sky. Presently they came to the end of the tram-lines and took the quiet mountain road,

139

and while the dew-cold air breathed out from the hedges they talked and planned and argued. The moon rose slowly in the sky and below them they could see the scattered lights of the city and a red neon sign expanding and contracting its barometer of light. They would feel then that they would be always happy. But a stray word about the old woman sets them squabbling and a sullen silence comes between them. Seeing he has hurt her Hugh takes her in his arms and she, holding the lapels of his coat, says in a whisper: 'Hugh, we must have patience!'

'All right, I'll not mention her again,' he promises.

She squeezed his hand and sighed when he kissed her.

They stood at a wooden gate looking at a moonlit stubble field, chill and bare, and hay hanging from the hedges where the laden carts had brushed past. They stood without speaking, enjoying the peace of the night, and watching the moon wriggle and break amongst the rushes in the Springfield Dam.

'Everything looks lovely at night,' said Eileen. 'The moon doesn't show up the filth the way the sun does.'

Suddenly a motor stretches its triangle of light between the hedges, and they turn their eyes from the blinding glare, feel the stir of the wind when the darkness swept in behind it, and for a time see nothing only the red tail-light boring into the funnel of the road. They turn for home again, their steps slow and lingering, and Hugh struggling to keep back the words that might crush their mood of peace.

It was late when he got back. The fire was out and the only light in the kitchen was the wavering glow from the oil lamp as it burned before the picture of the Sacred Heart. On the table were two pieces of bread and a cup of milk, a saucer covering its mouth. He lit the gas. The house was very quiet.

The lark yawned and stretched a wing. Lying on the sideboard were Mary's scissors, a needle with white thread and a pile of folded handkerchiefs covered lightly with brown paper. He sat at the table and took the bread and milk. Through the thin wall to the left he heard one of the McCormicks rhyming: 'I wan' a drink of water! I wan' a drink of water!' and Stick, himself, thumping at the foot of the stairs: 'Ye'll get no drink at this hour of the night. Go to sleep or I'll drink ye with the belt!' The noise subsided, the clock ticked, and from the wee room the springs of the bed creaked as the old woman turned.

Out in the street a drunk man was singing 'The Felons of Our Land' and Hugh knew it was Jackie McCloskey. He turned off the gaslight, for he didn't want him babbling at the door, and asking for a handful of scallions. Quietly he unlaced his boots, took them in his hand, and went up to bed.

Chapter XIII

Every day when the sun shone and when the children had come from school Hugh could see the old woman taking them up to the sloping fields above the brick yard. There she had discovered a sheltered hollow over topped by a thorn bush, reminding her of a hedgy stone in the country where she used to rest with her basket on a summer's day. She always carried pieces of bread for the children and a bottle of water which she pushed into the shade at the foot of the bush. She would spread a newspaper on the grass and take out her knitting from a green canvas work-bag which Mary had made for her. The little girls would peel off their stockings and run barefooted in the cool grass, resting now and then to make daisy chains or to hold buttercups under each other's chins.

141

While they played she sometimes rested her knitting on her lap and gazed down at the city — plunged in a haze of smoke, its throbbing noise muffled in the summerheat. She could see the sluggish river, the wasteground with white clothes swaying on the lines, and Johnny's fence with a yellow tin advertisement showing clearly. A longing for the country would infect her mind, and it was Lena coming back for a drink of water that would notice the tears in her eyes.

'Granny, you were crying?' she would say taking the cork from the bottle of water.

'I wasn't child — the grass makes me sneeze. Run on now and play,' and she would watch the shining bubbles racing from the mouth of the bottle.

In the evening the sun would wheel round, the bush lean its shadow in the hollow, and shreds of sunlight flicker upon her lap. Stiffly and reluctantly she would rise, lift the newspaper with the two middle fingers of one hand, and call the children. Carrying bunches of buttercups they would run to her and sit on the crushed grass to put on their shoes. Above their heads the sun shone, revealing on the bush a red piece of rotting rag. One evening the old woman saw it and a vision of Church Island on the Bann came to her — the water jabbling on the black stones of the shore, the gulls' feathers on the short grass, and on the tree that sheltered St. Patrick's stone pilgrims' rags drooping from the branches. She walked home in silence. Lena took her arm, Ann carried the work-bag, and Rita the empty bottle. They kept up a senseless chatter, and pointed to Hugh who was wheeling his barrow towards the drying shed. But her mind was on another world.

At the bridge that crossed the river Mary came to meet them, taking Oliver by the hand.

'Your daddy's back from the country,' she greeted, and they all scampered over the bridge, leaving the granny with Mary and Oliver.

Johnny observed the great change in his mother, and she holding his hands felt how hard they were from the pulling of the flax.

'Did you get much for your week?' she asked.

'Fifteen shillings and a load of turf.'

'Have you anything for me?'

'I have!' and her eyes brightened when he produced a bottle of poteen.

'Only for it I'd be dead long ago. It keeps the life in me,' she used to say as she rose from her rocking-chair after sipping the poteen out of a mug. She would slam the door of the wee room and stow the bottle safely away in one of her trunks.

'Don't slam that door,' Kate said to her one day, 'or you'll knock the delf off that shelf.'

'Oh, I didn't know you had delf up there,' and she looked at the shelf above the door.

'Well, you know now!' Kate said sharply. And that evening the old woman went off to bed early, banged the door behind her, and knocked down an egg-cup which smashed on the floor; later when Mary went in to sleep with her the granny abused her and told her that she kicked too much. Mary was patient with her, and to all her irritable gibes she remained silent.

The following morning when the dawn had crushed the darkness from the window and scattered the stars from the sky the old woman got up and announced to Mary that she was going to Mass. She went out by the back, and the astonished blackbirds flew up from amongst the vegetables in the garden and swayed on the fence. The dew lay like a heavy frost on the felt of the goat's shed and soaked the cabbage leaves. The silver wheel of a cobweb hung from the fence and drops clung to the bare clothes-lines. The whole city was asleep and through the silence she could hear the snoring pump of the brick yard draining water from the pit. She climbed to the thorn tree, her shoes wet, the grass sticking to them. She saw the sun rise, saddles of mist fall from the mountain, and smoke curl up from the houses. Over the roof-tops sounded the bells of the Monastery, and she hurried down from the field, following her tracks in the dew.

When she came back from Mass she was ill-humoured and hit Frankie on the head with her stick: 'I'll put the lies out of your head, my play actor.'

'Why, what did I do?' he asked, with an arm crooked above his head.

'You told me this was my pension day.'

'I did not!'

'You did!' and she went muttering into her room and banged the door.

When the children had gone to school she appeared for her breakfast and took a tantrum of calling Johnny by the name 'Andy'. He paid no heed to her and she flared up: 'Well, why don't you answer?'

'If you don't call me by my right name I'll not answer for the wrong one,' he replied, and then seeking some excuse he went out, called the dog, and set off up through the fields near the mountain to gather mushrooms.

When he came back in the afternoon she was in bed. He carried a fresh sod for the lark and a handkerchief filled with mushrooms. Kate stewed the mushrooms with butter and pepper, toasted a round of bread at the bars of the grate, and made tea for the old woman.

'Johnny tramped miles to gather them for you,' she said.

'I knew I smelt them, but I thought I imagined it. Ah, Kate, that earthy smell of a mushroom fairly lifts my heart.'

She rocked herself on the arm-chair, and she was stroking the white cat and singing to herself when

144

Hugh came in from work. As he washed at the jar-tub he felt that it wouldn't be long now till she would pack her trunks and bid good-bye to the city. In his walk with Eileen he arranged the marriage for Christmas, but she was afraid to hope too much and refused to enthuse with him about the future.

'Why don't you look forward to everything,' he advised her. 'Even if it doesn't happen — well, you've got the pleasure of dreaming about it now.'

'I know, Hugh, I know, but it's the disappointment that's hard to bear. Supposing she does go back to the country — what about Mary? She might change her mind about the convent, and not go at all.'

'Mary's only waiting on the word. She has all prepared — she might be going next week!' and he talked so convincingly that at last Eileen was engulfed in his belief and she held the lapels of his coat, looked up at him with great tenderness and told him how she had been gathering in secret a few things that they might need.

He whistled as he walked home in the August night. He came up to the waste ground and saw the light of a flash-lamp in the garden — his father out catching slugs. Furtively he looked over the fence. His father was groping amongst the cabbage leaves and searching under the small stones of the soil. His mother followed, holding the flash-lamp and an empty jam-jar.

'Be patient with her,' Johnny was saying. 'Them fits of temper is not a good sign. If she takes a notion for the country the devil couldn't hold her back.' He stretches out a handful of slugs and she holds holds up the jam-jar to receive them. 'She could never look after herself. Lena's too young, and Mary — well, she'll be away in the convent. I trust in God she'll stick it.'

Kate blows her nose; and the light from the lamp

145

wheels across the garden. They stoop again; the light brightens their pink hands and faces, glints on the brass eyeholes of Johnny's boots, and creases his trousers with shadow.

' 'Deed she'll stick it, Johnny. They'll not get a better, good-living girl than our Mary.' She sees a slug and drops it into the jar. 'She's nearly blinded with that hemstitching. Her eyes be very raw in the mornings.'

'A rest and good nourishing food will cure them.' His penknife drops on the soil; Kate dips the lamp till he picks it up. He puts his fingers through the holes in a cabbage leaf.

'They've had a square feed out of that cabbage. Such havoc! I must lime the soil well — it's a bit on the sour side.'

The light in the lamp grows dim and Kate gives it a shake.

'I'm afraid the battery's on its last legs, Johnny.'

'We're nearly done for the night. I just want to pull a few scallions for Liza and Jackie — they've been decent with us.'

The lamp flickers and goes out. Hugh turns quietly from the fence and goes into the house.

Chapter XIV

'We'll go this way, Mother,' Mary was saying as they crushed their way into the open-air variety market where Mary intended to buy a few things for the children before leaving for the convent.

There was no order amongst the crowds. The sun blazed from a blue sky, and the bundles of old clothes spread out on the counters exuded a warm, sour smell. Women with baskets jostled one another around the stalls, tramping on damaged fruit, lingering here to watch a man punching holes in a basin and mending them while-you-wait with liquid solder, or a little man standing on a high box, a hand thrust into a silk stocking, and with many flourishes of his wrist demonstrating the uses of his mend-the-ladder needle: 'Ladies, one moment. I'm not here to sell these needles, I'm here to advertise them! . . . See, I pluck a ladder in this stocking. Now watch closely to see how this simply worked needle can mend it . . . a baby in arms could use it . . . See . . . as good as new,' and he waves the stocking in front of the ladies' faces. 'Of course if there is any young lady in the audience would like one, I'll oblige her. Sixpence each! Though as I said before and I repeat again — I'm not here to sell these needles, I'm here to advertise them. I've only a few with me . . . Sixpence . . . Thank you, ladies. Money refunded if not satisfactory.'

'I'm afraid, Mary, you'll not need one of them gadgets where you're going,' and they pushed towards a clothes-stall where Kate bargained over a boy's coat that had a hole in the sleeve. She got it for a shilling.

'It'll do Frankie for the winter. I'll patch it and give it a good washing and airing.'

The stall-owner folded her arms when Kate asked her to wrap the coat in brown paper. 'No paper supplied on articles under a shilling,' she said to Kate, pursing her lips and shaking her head haughtily. 'Wrap it in brown paper! Not a newspaper, mind you! But the very best of brown paper.'

Mary reddened and moved off, but Kate out of spite lingered at the stall, pretending to be interested in other wares. Farther along a decrepit old woman sold her a pair of men's trousers for two shillings; they were navy blue, the flaps slightly frayed, and one brown button sewed on the back with white thread.

A man with one arm, the loose sleeve tucked neatly into a pocket of his coat, was selling perfumed soap, and Kate had compassion on him and bought from him a fresh bar of soap for the old woman. Up between the aisles of stalls they pushed, grateful for the little breeze that eddied the thick heat or swayed the shadows of the hanging clothes. Shawled women sat on empty boxes, their wares spread out at their feet — old ornaments, brass fenders, portmanteaux with foreign labels and blue-moulded fastenings, boots in all stages of decomposition, and cups and bowls with straw and dust in them. A man in evening dress was selling wild nettle juice for bronchitis, wild carrot juice for eye diseases, and ivy paint for the complete removal of corns, while behind him his coloured charts creaked in the wind and a large design, in relief, announced to all over fifty that they would die of cancer if they did not take a course of Dr. Zachery's White Powder.

Suddenly Mary halted and pinched her mother's arm.

'What is it?' said Kate. But already Mary was smiling to the two scraggy sisters who had lived so mysteriously at the top of the street. They had a stall of their own and pushed in at the side was the pram the waterproof sheet folded neatly over the handle. They specialized in ladies' frocks, the best of which hung from coat-hangers, the prices pinned to the tail.

'Granny used to torment me about them,' Mary said. 'She always wondered where they went with their pram on Friday morning. They're hard workers.'

'They've their wits about them. I'm sure they make a good penny out of this business. They deserve to get on well.'

Mary bought a hair-clasp for Lena, a tiny basket for Ann, and a picture book for Rita; and at a grocery stall Kate got a dozen of chipped eggs at half-price. Two of the young McCormicks passed them carrying empty boxes, and Kate gave them a penny to buy sweets. They were elbowing their way

148

towards the gate when they met Eileen Curran, a laden basket in her hand, out of which stuck a bronze ornament, and under her arm a picture of the Holy Family with the glass cracked in one corner. She blushed when she saw them, and Mary noticing her embarrassment was the first to speak:

'We're meeting everybody to-day,' she said. 'Isn't the air here very close?'

Eileen was conscious of Kate's eyes riveted on the basket. She tried to edge it to the side and keep the face of the picture turned inwards.

'The people here would knock you down,' she said, stepping to the side of a stall where the shafts of a handcart diverted the moving crowd. They chatted for a few minutes, Eileen contriving to distract their attention from the basket and the picture. But Mary was aware of her restlessness and the disconcerted movement of her eyes. She smiled: 'We must move on now, Eileen. You'll be up to see me before I go away.'

Kate remained silent till they had reached the fresh freedom of the open streets.

'Mary, did you see the picture and the ornament in her basket? Would Hugh be getting married, do you think?'

'He'd tell us. Eileen might have got the picture cheap and taken a fancy to it.'

'It wouldn't suit us if Hugh ran off and took his good pay with him,' and now that she had given utterance to a thought which for a long time had been troubling her she wanted to rush home and to talk with Hugh until he confessed what was in his mind.

'God knows — if the old woman wasn't there!' she muttered to herself.

'What's that you say, Mother?'

'Nothing, girl, nothing. I'm counting up what we've spent,' and suddenly the basket with the eggs, the coat, and the trousers seemed to have become very heavy.

When they got home Rita was sitting on the sofa crying. She was sticking out her tongue and the grandmother was giving her sips of cold water. Oliver was riding on the rocking-horse which Frankie had carried down from the landing. The greyhound was lying at the fender, and Lena and Ann were dressed-up and playing 'shop'.

'Such a house!' said Kate, leaving the basket on the table. 'What's wrong with Rita?'

'They have my head astray since you left,' the granny said wearily. 'She plagued the life out of me for a clove, and I give her a bit of one I was chewing and it burned her tongue.'

Mary handed her the story book and she ceased crying; Frankie was ordered up the stairs again with the rocking-horse; the greyhound was put out in the yard; and in a few minutes the house was at peace again. Kate mended the sleeve of the coat and put it in a bath to steep; then she searched the pockets of the navy trousers and found a spent match and a safety pin. She hung the trousers out on the line to take the mouldy smell off them.

Mary ransacked her cardboard boxes which contained an accumulation of Christmas cards, buttons, sequins, holy pictures, broken rosary beads, and religious medals. Lena, Ann, and Rita sat beside her stretching out their hands and pleading for the coloured Christmas cards, and Mary would give one to each in rotation, then sometimes she would re-read an old letter, crumple it in her hands and throw it into the fire. Soon she had given away every little thing that had belonged to her, and felt there was nothing more to do before leaving for the convent except to take her leave of the neighbours.

Next evening her friends crowded in to see her, each asking her to pray for a special intention, and Liza McCloskey whispering to her not to forget poor Jackie and the pledge. Kate made tea and they

150

sang and danced until midnight. The old woman sat silent in her arm-chair, stroking the cat, and occasionally poking the fire; and once when a strange silence had fallen upon the company she sang in a husky, quavery voice:

> 'Oh, calm is yon lake and thrice calm is yon river,
> I've roamed by the Tiber, the Seine, and the Clyde.
> I've seen the Ohio roll forth in it splendour
> But my heart longs to be by the Bann's waterside.'

Before she had finished the song Kate stole out by the back and walked up and down the waste ground, seeing the smoky beams of light above the yard walls and hearing the river purling around the stones. She yawned and felt the cold night air. She told herself what with Mary's departure the house would never be the same, and as she pondered on it, and then thought of Peter away in the Home and of Hugh's silent hostility towards the old woman she sighed wearily. Someone called to her and turning round she saw Johnny outlined in the rectangle of light at the backdoor. She walked towards him keeping her head sideways to the light so that he wouldn't notice she had been crying.

'What are you doing, Kate?'

'I thought I'd left clothes out on the line,' and for a while they stood in silence looking at the light from the door stretching to the garden gate and reflecting on the brass padlock.

Behind them came the scraggy notes of a mouth-organ. Two of the McCormicks were dancing in their bare feet, their father playing for them as he sat on the sofa, the old woman beating time on the bars of the grate with the poker. The boys pirouetted simultaneously, clapped their bare ankles,

151

turned back to back, their feet working with sharp rapidity, and then with grotesque movements of their hands and legs they bowed and sat tailor-like on the floor.

'What's the name of that dance?' put in Jackie McCloskey after he had applauded.

'It all came out of my own head,' Stick answered proudly.

'Well, it's damned good — damned good,' Jackie said absent-mindedly, 'and they never made one mistake. They're two right wee dancers!'

Kate fussed about, carrying the tea-pot and urging the timid visitors to eat. Sometimes she would withdraw to the darkness of the scullery and gaze into the lighted kitchen, at the tobacco smoke swirling under the gas-globe, the lark wide-awake in his cage, and Mary sitting on the edge of the table, her white handkerchief tucked into the sleeve of her black dress, her pale face distraught with quiet weariness. Liza was sitting on the fender reading with affected solemnity the cups that were being passed to her: seeing in a young wife's the safe arrival of a pair of twins — each announcement being greeted with a burst of laughter.

It was after midnight when the company broke up, Liza remaining for awhile to help to clean up the dishes. Mary went to bed but she could not sleep, and in the morning she was up first, lit the fire, and made the breakfast. But the children could eat nothing, dazed as they were from the previous night's excitement and burdened now with an imminent parting which they could not fully understand. Mary tried to be cheerful — humming songs to herself, brushing the dust from under the chest of drawers, and arranging the chairs about the table. Her mother, her head thrust forward, busied herself about the scullery, glancing at the clock whenever she passed through the kitchen. Then she went upstairs and brought a suit-case down with her, and in silence Mary went into the wee room and put on a black coat and hat.

'Close the door, Mary, like a good girl,' said the old woman, 'and sit on the bed and talk to me.'

Mary sat down, her forefinger tracing a square on the patchwork quilt. The old woman took her hand and pressed it firmly to her breast: 'May God take care of you and give you the strength and grace to stick it!' She stroked her hand: 'When you're made a nun I'll not be here . . . You'll pray for me? . . .'

Mary's lips quivered; she turned her head and saw in the fireplace the piece of frilled green paper dusted with soot. The curtains swayed and a white feather was blown across the floor.

Mary took her handkerchief from her sleeve: 'Don't be fretting, granny . . . I'm happy . . . Only for you . . . coming to the city . . . I wouldn't be able to go.' She wiped her eyes. 'I'll write to you.' And standing up she saw three match-strokes on the blue wall.

In the kitchen she spoke loudly to her father, to Frankie, and her little sisters. Oliver was bent over the suit-case fingering its silver fastenings. She took him in her arms and kissed him; then she patted the dog's head, and not wanting to take her leave of the neighbours again she went out by the waste ground her mother carrying the suit-case. She passed the little bridge at the river and Hugh, who was looking out for her, paused in his work to wave to her.

Once on to the tram a numbness came over her. She could think of nothing; and in a mournful dreaminess saw the familiar hoardings with their coloured advertisements and heard the faint punching of the tickets and the rattle of the coppers in the conductor's bag. She went to the Home to see Peter, but of that farewell visit she could recall but little — save that he had grown tall, that he had given her a tiny boot which he had made himself, and that he had said nothing to her except to ask for the loan of sixpence.

In the train which was taking her to the convent her mother sat silent in the corner and she, finding no words to say to her, tried to take an interest in the scenes that flashed past the window: the sun flashing on a canal, a man on top of a hayrick waving to them, a can lying against a stook of corn — but always Peter with his black nervous eyes would confront her, or the heart-breaking journey it must have been for the old woman when she was leaving her home in the country.

During her second day in the convent when she was rubbing the clothes-line to take off the rust, prior to hanging out the washing, that visit to Peter shattered her mind and tormented her like a sin. She told herself that it was she who was to blame for his stubborn silence. She remembered how she had held out the tiny boot in the palm of her hand and how she in her desire to get away from the Home had been abrupt with him when he wanted to tell her how he had made it. He had relapsed into a subdued inertness and it was his mother who had tried to cheer him:

'Do you like to be in the Home, Peter?' she had asked.

'It's all right.'

'Would you like to be home again, son?'

'Sometimes.'

After that they had said good-bye. She recalled how she had taken his hand and how he had looked away from her with a pained smile.

It was her selfishness was to blame she told herself. God knows if she would ever see him again or be able to do something kind to him. She sighed deeply. The clothes flapped on the line. Below her a train tore its smoke above the hedges and she turned her back on it, renouncing the little pleasure a wave of a hand from a carriage window might give her.

Chapter XV

A week after Mary's departure to the convent the
sun had come out strong, though it was mid-
September, and the children pestered the old
woman to take them up the fields to the thorn
bush.

'Don't stay too long,' Kate called after them.
'It gets cold now in the evenings.'

They set off — the old woman with her stick
and green canvas work-bag, Lena walking beside
her, and Ann and Rita running in front. They
passed over the bridge across the river, and climbed
the sloping field to the thorn bush. As usual she
spread a newspaper in the hollow and took out her
knitting while the children scattered to the hedges
to gather blackberries.

Around her dockens were rusting with seed,
clumps of nettles were charred with decay, and
sparrows picked at the seeding groundsel. But the
birds were silent. Above her head the varnished sunlight shone on the smitten leaves of the bush and
glowed on the red haws which clotted the branches.
Flocks of crows, black and glossy with harvest
health, alighted clumsily in the field and waddled
about till the shouts of the children scattered them.
The old woman rested her knitting on her lap and
watched the ragged flight of the crows and listened
to their disorderly cawing as they perched in a
clump of trees.

The children's faces were purpled and streaked
with the juice of blackberries, and Ann and Rita
were holding out their bare arms showing how the
briars had scratched them. They all sat on the
outspread newspapers, but when the granny took
a fine comb from her apron pocket Lena moved
away from her laughing: 'Do Rita's first, she's the
youngest.' As she carefully unwrapped the fine
comb from its covering of brown paper she pretended

155

not to hear the remark, then she said casually to Lena: 'Lena, child, get me a thimble out of the work-bag,' and when Lena came close to her she caught her by the leg: 'Now, Miss Smarty, I'll do you first.' Lena smiled, put her head down on her granny's lap and surrendered to the comb. She tried to keep still, at the same time plaguing the old woman with questions about nuns and convents.

'I was in a convent myself,' said granny, her eyes following the progress of the comb.

The children stared at her and remained quiet, waiting for her to say something more.

'But were you a nun like our Mary?' Lena asked impatiently.

'No, child, I was not,' she went on slowly. 'I was only seven at the time. My mother was a cook in a big house and my father — God be good to him — was dead, and I was sent in to the nuns. I remember the outside of the building, for it had a big, big picture of the Holy Family above the gate' — and she demonstrated the size of the picture with a sweep of her hands — 'My mother used to come up at night — that was the time she got off her work — but I never saw her because I was asleep. But I always knew when she was there, for there was always an apple or sweets for me the next day.'

'And did you see the nuns?' Lena asked, raising her head from her lap.

'There was a wee nun I liked very much,' she replied, pushing down Lena's head again and raking it with the fine comb. 'She was as thin and delicate as a candle. When I met her in the corridor at nine o'clock in the morning she always took an egg for me out of her pocket. The egg was cold then and I always went into a corner and peeled the shell off it and ate it, and I always dropped the shells in a flower-pot that stood on a mahogany stand. And then I'd go up to a room away at the top of the building and from a window I could see the green

156

fields and the twists in a canal. And on the canal there was a bridge and when a boat hooted I ran to the window for I knew the bridge was going to swing open and I'd see the boat and the waves spreading out behind her.'

'But did you play any games?' said Lena, rising to her feet. Ann knelt down and took her place.

'We did play games,' and she looked at Ann's ears and tut-tutted at the dirt in them. 'And on Reverend Mother's birthday we always had a little sing-song. We had paper dresses and bonnets and we carried stools and sang about cows. And one Christmas I was dressed as an angel with two white wings. But a little girl closed the door on my wings and broke them. I was sent to bed, but I was brought back again and my wings were mended with sticking-plaster and I went on the stage and sang: "See amid the Winter's Snow".'

Suddenly everything had become very quiet. A grey cloud obscured the sun and down in the brick yard the bogies lay motionless on the silver rails.

'It's late, children,' and she felt the chill breath of the grass. She folded her knitting and slowly straightened her back. She sniffed the cold air : 'We should have been home an hour ago!' And as she moved off she asked Lena to take her hand. Near the dumps Kate came to meet them, carrying a heavy shawl in her hands.

'What on earth kept you? You'll get your death — the lot of you,' and she wrapped the shawl about the old woman. Lena began to retell the stories about the nuns, but her mother wasn't listening to her. She was thinking of Hugh and was relieved, when they reached the house, to find that he had finished his tea and had gone out.

With Mary gone a growing grudge towards the old woman manifested itself: Hugh was sudden in his silences, he was curt in his behaviour towards her, and he stubbornly refused to go in to see her if she had retired early to her room. Towards his mother he was also moody, but she took the easy way with him, hoping that his fits of bad temper would pass. But since the day she had met Eileen in the market nothing would dissuade her that they intended to get married soon. The thought worried her. At night she would lie awake talking to herself — What if Hugh did leave the house? Sure we got on very well without him before he got this job. Poor Mary was a loss to us — but it's God's will. And Johnny — he's a good man but a bit headstrong. Many a good penny he'd have made with his hand-cart if he hadn't struck the hotel porter; it's better to put your pride in your pocket. Anyway, maybe he'll arrive home with a few more shillings from the harvesting. Her mind would relax, she would sigh to herself in the darkness and watch the light from the street-lamp slanting below the blind and smoothing the frame of a picture. Then her mind would start again in its mad eddying whirl and she would recall the day the bailiffs arrived at the house and the night the policeman took Peter away. Later she would fall into a restless sleep, her arm around one of the children who slept with her.

To-night after making punch for the old woman, because she had remained up the fields too long, her mind was more perturbed than usual. Oliver was restless and once or twice he had cried out in his sleep and she had tip-toed over to the cot and patted his head. Then back again to her own bed where she blessed herself and tried in God's name to sleep. She thought she heard the old woman cry out and she raised her head from the pillow and listened. Her heart thumped. She heard Frankie stir and the wire mattress creaking. She lay back again; then like a clock that is running down her mind jolted in its widening span. 'What'll Johnny say if she has got a chill?' she asked herself.

158

She lit a candle, and with a shawl over her nightdress went quietly down the stairs. She noticed a crack of light below the door of the wee room, and going in saw the old woman standing on the floor, bending over the bed and brushing the sheet. Kate withdrew, coughed, and made a noise in the kitchen. She pushed open the door again and the old woman looked at her.

'What in God's name is wrong?' said Kate, noticing how the face was wrinkled and pinched with cold.

'I can't sleep! It's the bed — Oliver must have ate a biscuit in it. The sheet's covered with wee hard lumps and they're cutting the hinches off me.'

Kate took a coat from a nail in the door and put it round the old woman's shoulders, and then to put her at her ease she brushed the sheet stiffly and pretended to throw crumbs from her palm into the grate. 'Now get in, there isn't a speck left in it.' The old woman shivered, shrugged her shoulders, and blew out her breath with the cold.

'There's a heavy frost the night and I can't get warm. My poor bones are prodding me.'

'Have you enough clothes on?' said Kate, stretching a hand below the blankets and groping for the hot water bottle. 'I'll fill the bottle up again and bring you a nice warm drink.'

She closed the window, pinned another shawl on her, and then when she had settled down she blew out the candles and took away the matches from the room.

All the next day the granny remained gathered-up in bed, the clothes over her head. She was silent and ate nothing. Liza McCloskey came in, but to all her cheery loud-voiced gossip and forced laughs the old woman was listless.

At night she complained bitterly of the cold. 'Kate,' she would say. 'There's no heat in my blood and my bones are jagging me. I'm cold-rifed. I feel

as if someone is pouring spring water down my back.'
Father Teelan visited her and tried to cheer her with
jokes about the country and the making of poteen.
'Do they still make the poteen in Lough Beg?' he
would say. 'Man, Mrs. Griffin, if you had a good
jorum of it it would put you on your feet again.'

Then one evening she heard Kate and Hugh arguing
aloud in the kitchen. The door was ajar and she
heard Hugh shouting: 'She could go up to the Union.
She'd be better off there than here!'

'Hugh!' said his mother and she had looked at him
with despair.

'She could go to the Union!' he repeated again.

Kate poked the fire gently: Hugh, son, under God,
what hardness has come over you? The Workhouse!
— I'd rather be in my grave than see her there!'

'There's better than her in it! They're well looked
after.' His voice was hard. He sat on the sofa
bending down to brush his boots. His mother said
nothing and her silence irritated him. He would
thrash it out now.

'If she doesn't go you'll not have me any longer!
I've warned you about this before.'

'Hugh, you'll come to no good,' and she rubbed
her hands together, and seeing the door of the wee
room ajar she went and closed it.

He raised his head, flinging back his long black
hair from his brow. He held the boot brush in his
hand and glared at his mother.

'I'm going to get married, and either I go or she
goes!'

'What in God's name can I do! It was to help us
that she left her good home in the country. Only
for her pension we'd been out in the street long ago
like a pack of tramps.'

'Her pension helped us very little. She ates most
of it herself. What thanks have I got for slaving to
keep the fire in the grate for the past six months?'

She hated to hear the hard stoniness of his

voice: 'Who kept it for all the years you were at school! Who fed you and clothed you and kept shoes on your feet! And now you turn in to boss the house!'

'Who's trying to boss the house!' he blazed. 'There's no peace in it! There's no comfort in it since that old woman came into it. She can go back now or else go up to the Workhouse!' He stood up, straightened his tie, and lit a cigarette.

'Can't you wait for a little while?' she said quietly taking the easy way. 'God knows she'll not be long for this earth and we may show her some kindness while she's in it.'

'I'm sick listening to that word "wait". I've waited long enough . . . Is she going or am I?'

'She's not!'

'All right!'

'You'll live to regret this — no good ever came out of bad temper.'

He ran up the stairs and packed his clothes in a brown paper parcel. When he came down his mother was sitting on a chair at the fire, her hands resting wearily on her lap.

'I'm going and I'm not coming back!'

She covered her eyes with her hand and shook her head. He stood with his back to her looking out of the window at the children playing in the street and the lamp-lighter passing with his yellow pole. He waited for his mother to say something, then he turned and saw that the door of the wee room had opened. The old woman was standing in the doorway, the red flannel cowled over her head, the heavy nightdress wrinkled about her ankles. Her face was dead except for her eyes. She dragged herself across to the arm-chair and sat down.

Hugh gazed dumbly at her and saw the print of her bare feet on the tiles. She seemed to have grown smaller. Not until now had he perceived how wasted she was: the shrunken face, the whiteness of her hair under the red flannel, the knuckled deformity of her feet. She coughed and clutched the black shawl on her chest.

'You're fighting about me!' she said brokenly. 'God forgive me for bringing strife into any house!'

'We're not,' Kate lied to her and put her arm round her shoulders. 'We're not indeed. Come back to bed like a good woman or you'll get your death.'

'Hugh, come here to me,' and from under the fringe of shawl she stretched out her thin, withered arm.

He was suddenly afraid of her. 'I'll not! I'll not!' and he lifted his parcel and ran out.

She bowed her head and rocked the chair. She remembered the day he had come out of prison and she had asked him to come to her — then, too, she had been sitting on the chair and he standing at the window.

She shook her head: 'Och, och, the people is all different. Their natures is hard and dry as flint!'

The lark flitted, shaking the cage. The dusk was gathering at the window. The kettle on the fire boiled over and hissed on the coals, and Kate gripped the handle with her apron and lifted it on to the hob.

'Come now and I'll make you a hot cup of tea,' and as she helped her to her room she could feel the sharp fleshless bones and the coldness of her body.

'Where has Hugh gone? It was me that vexed him.'

'No, Granny,' Kate lied again. 'What put that in your head! He's away to pawn his new suit. Didn't you see it in the parcel? He doesn't like the colour of it. I warned him that he'd lose a power of money on it, but he wouldn't listen to me. He's a bit head-strong.'

'Ai, ai,' she replied, her mind shattered with the scraps of conversation she had overheard. 'I'm a burden to you all. The Workhouse! The Workhouse! May God hasten my end!'

162

'Hush, hush, sure nobody was talking about the Workhouse!'

'I know, I know,' and as she leaned her head on the pillow she closed her eyes and wept.

'We're glad to have you here! We'll always be glad to have you!' and Kate took her hands and pressed them with intense fervour.

'Johnny will always stand by me!'

'He will! He will!' Kate assured her and sat on the bed watching the grey sky crouching at the window. Then she heard the dog scratch at the back door and she went to let him in, and stood for a minute watching the evening fall.

A yellow light haloed the top of the mountain and the smoke of dusk gathered over the waste ground and lay thick in the hollows of the river. The water jabbled around the quoins of the arch and a flock of gulls lay at the top of the smoking dumps. Presently one of them arose, flew down to the river, and alighted on the top of a half-submerged box; it swayed unsteadily for a moment, slowly folded its wings and began to preen itself, a few of its feathers, light as thistle seed, floating away in the air. Everything was quiet and at peace, but her own mind was crunched with sorrow, squeezed and spent after that scene with Hugh, and she was afraid to ask herself would he come back. She stood inert and weary. The dusk crept into the corners of the brick yard, and the yellow sky smoked with the approach of night. In the dim light the garden seemed neglected: a tattered sack drooped from the broken wire and a piece of paper clung to the black wooden gate. 'Hugh doesn't take after his father,' she sighed to herself, 'or he'd mend that fence before the children pulled it down.' The white cat pressed out from under the gate, ran into the yard and hopped on to the window sill of the wee room. Kate bolted the yard door and went into the kitchen.

In a stunned, listless manner she got the children

to bed and while she was cleaning their shoes in readiness for the next morning she often paused in her work to peer up and down the street. Then she sat in the light of the fire, her hands on her lap, their palms upward. The tap dripped in the scullery, but she made no move to turn it off. At eleven o' clock she put on her coat and walked down to Eileen Curran's. A light shone in the window, and as she stood at the door hesitating she heard a burst of women's laughter. Furtively she sped away, came back home, left the door ajar, and on the table place a mug of milk and buttered bread.

She fell on her knees at the bedside to say her prayers, and then without taking off her clothes lay on top of the quilt. The stairs creaked; the child whimpered in his sleep — to each minute sound she raised her head. How long the night was! She heard the clock strike. Then the front door was pushed open and a wind zoomed through the house. She heard the fumbling of matches, the rasp of the emery on a matchbox, and the pock of the gas as it was lighted. Later there was the smell of a cigarette.

Chapter XVI

For three days the old woman had eaten nothing and complained of the stony coldness of her body. Her brown eyes were glazed a milky white, and from her bed she saw the sky covered with grey clouds and heard the rainy winds blowing in gusts against the pane. The rain would whip-lash the window and she would see the bare clothes-line swaying in the yard or listen to the forlorn rattling of the loose tin on Johnny's fence. Lights were lit early in the day and Kate would bring a candle into the room, spill a few grease drops upon the mantelpiece and stick the candle down on them. And to the old woman's question about the time Kate would always reply that it was five o'clock.

'Ah, Kate,' she would answer, 'the winter's here and I'll never see another.' She would watch Kate go out and the candle flame smudging the blue wall when a draught rushed through the room.

The days dragged, brightened now and then when Father Teelan called in the mornings to give her Holy Communion. But when the children came in from school she would have to rap the wall at them and order them to keep quiet. Sometimes Oliver would give a sharp cry and she would think that he had fallen into the fire, and her heart would flutter wildly and her breathing quicken.

But it was Johnny, when he had come back from the country, who shortened the nights for her. He would sit in the room and talk to her of the fields and how well he had pitted the potatoes for her: 'I've a good mortar of mould and rushes on the north side of the pit. There isn't a black blowing frost could penetrate it.' She in turn would ask endless questions about the house: 'Is there any sign of moss on the thatch? . . . Did any of them auction men paste bills on the door? . . . Did you pin the brown paper on the dresser shelves? . . . Did you naphtha flake the bed? . . . Did you inquire about the hens?' and she would follow in her own mind the action which accompanied each of these little chores, and sigh frequently, for cloistered within her mind was the prescience of death and the memory of the graves which she knew he had visited. And day after day her rosary would pass through her haggard fingers and she would pray for those she may have led into sin, and pray also to God for the grace of a happy death.

One evening she crawled out of bed and opened her two trunks. She delved amongst the smell of camphor, scrutinizing sheaves of small grocery accounts — afraid, perhaps, that one was left unpaid. She fingered an old spectacle case which was stripped of it leather covering, its purple velvet lining stained with yellow snuff; she tried to read the faded gilt lettering of the maker's name, but could make no sense of it nor could she remember how she had come to possess it. She put it back in the trunk and lifted up a black prayer book with its binding eaten to shreds by wood lice and its pages browned and specked with age. That, too, she put back, and then took out too beeswax candles wrapped in tissue paper and tied with a brown shoelace. She closed her trunks and pushed the candles under the pillow, thinking of the last time she had used them — at the deaths of her sons: Michael and Patrick.

Kate came in with tea and the old woman produced the candles: 'There's two blessed candles I found in my trunk. Take the pair, Kate, for I've more of my own at home. You never know when you might need them.'

And Kate aware of what was centred in her mind took the candles and unrolled the rustling tissue paper: ' 'Deed that's the truth, you never know when one of the neighbours might want to borrow them. I'll keep them in the chest of drawers in the kitchen.'

At this time Frankie earned many a penny. He went to the shop across the street for her snuff and for the baking soda which relieved her stomach pains, and many a time she would give him sweets when he would go to the chapel for her and light a candle at Our Lady's altar. And one day while he was filling her snuff box she whispered to him to close the door and taking his two hands she looked at him fiercely:

'Tell me the truth, Frankie: Does Hugh ever mention the Workhouse to your mother?'

'No, Granny, I never heard him!'

'Are you sure?' and she nipped his arm.

'As sure as God's in heaven I never heard him!'

'If he ever does, tell me, Frankie! Tell me!' and she lay back. 'If they do! . . . if they do! . . . I'll put a match to my bed! . . . No Griffin ever died in the Workhouse!'

The cold squally days turned to frost and chilled the air in the room. A fistful of fire was lit in the grate, fizzling all day under a coat of wet slack and choking the room with burnt smoke. The skies that framed the window were stitched with stars or sometimes streaked with cloud that glowed with a hazy light or crumbled into a flimsy texture when driven in front of the moon. In the morning the clothes-line in the yard, would be frozen and the bricks that topped the wall polished with thin ice. The sparrows, shrunken with cold, would hop over the icy bricks alighting sometimes on the clothes-line before descending to the yard there to pick around the drain amongst the brown tea leaves and wet bread crumbs. With an unutterable yearning the old woman would think of the wintry days in the country, the drops glistening on the starved hedges, the frost dripping from the thatch, and the hungry birds flitting at the window or nervously feeding with the hens.

The cold nights were killing her; her eyes became more sunken, her bones more pointed, and when she was tortured with pain her face would shrivel up and she would ask God to take her, and in the mornings say to Kate: 'It's only when you can't sleep, when there's no blood in you and your bones a burden that you thank God there's such a thing as death.'

They began to sit up with her, to keep watch — Johnny, one night; then Hugh, then Kate, and sometimes Liza or Stick's wife came in to relieve them. They knew it was nearing the end: her mind cut adrift and she raved aloud — 'They're good trunks, the best that money can buy: and Robert Emmet in his black cork frame singing: "She is far from the Land" — Why didn't he sing about the Bann — that's a nice patriot for you! Johnny was a good son to me — the best that money can buy. What am I talking about? My mind's rambling — that's what it's doing, rambling all over the demesne hunting for rabbits. Johnny and his rabbits! He never got me to eat any of them — they're full of tape worm.'

She saw Kate bring in two candlesticks and a saucer with bread crumbs which she placed on a white-clothed table; and amongst the scattered remnants of her crumbling mind she sought for something that would make sense of Kate's movements, but her mind was fallow, dried up with exhaustion, emaciated with sleeplessness.

That evening they all crowded in to say the rosary at her bedside, Johnny giving out the Hail Marys, the rest answering him. She raised herself on the pillow and stretched out her bare, wasted arm: 'As thin as a ruler,' she said and sank back on the pillow.

'Ye needn't be shouting,' she raved, 'for I can hear you rightly. And what are you lighting the candles for? . . . the room's bright enough since Johnny pulled down the ivy . . . Now that Doctor knows nothing — he's too young, and his wee chip of a moustache makes him look no older. Don't bring him here again or I'll affront him: putting two of Stick McCormick's boards on my wrist. What does he know about an old woman's aches and pains? Ai, I smelt drink off him — a nice way to come into a sick room. Give him a peppermint, Mary, or a clove — you'll get them there in my apron pocket that's hanging behind the door . . . What are you all mumbling about? Tell Peter to get me red wool and chickens out of the demesne. You're all whispering again, whispering — the whispering brook. Get me my hair-pins out of the trunk. Let in the cat, let it in, for I hear it scraping in the rat. I'm doting — a cat scraping in the rat.

That's the best ever I heard. Tell that one to Luke, the postman — a brave craythure. He likes a wee sup on a cold day. That's what drink done for my husband — he lost his fields — a foolish good-natured man. Who's that fornent the door? The wee black fellow — is that you, Peter, or is it old Nick, himself? Take a seat at the fire? it's a cold night and your famished. It'll soon warm you and all them candles lit. Extravagance — and them two for three-halfpence. There's the clocks, the clocks, the clocks — they're going to strike . . . .'

'Yer back again, Father Teelan, and you only away. Tell them to blow out the candles, Father, they're two for threehalfpence. Isn't that right?'

'That's right,' answered the priest.

'They're all mumbling, Father, but I can hear them. They think I'm deaf. Did I ever tell you about my gall stones, Father? They were as big as swan's eggs. They're down in Ballymena — nice people in Ballymena, they'd split a halfpenny; a nice place for Saint Patrick to herd pigs. Many's a time I seen him with his crozier at the spring well and the mud between his bare toes . . . Johnny, son, come here to me . . . .'

Johnny got up from his knees and put his hand on her forehead: 'This is Johnny. Do you feel me all right?'

'Don't shout, son. Get me my skirt and slippers till I get home out of this. Tell Mary to pack my trunks . . . Nobody hears me! Nobody hears me! . . .'

Hugh knelt beside the closed door, his head leaning against the coats and the shawls that hung from it. He drooped his head as he answered the prayers. She was dying now and he had never said a kind word to her. How often had he heard her say that to live for others was to live well. He combed his fingers through his hair. It all seemed very far away the wet day he had distempered the room to prepare for her coming.

'Johnny, son, don't go away! The sight is leaving me!' She gave a long moan.

The children began to cry and Kate brought them quietly from the room. They tiptoed up the stairs and Ann asked Lena if her granny would see the angels to-night. 'Sh-sh-sh,' said Lena, and she in turn remembered the story her granny had told her about mending the angel's wings with sticking-plaster.

Frankie stood at the window and undressed in the light of the street lamp she shone in. The snow had fallen and the roofs, the sills, and the window-sashes were hushed with its quiet softness. He could see a few flakes falling in disorder around the arms of the lamp-post, and saw black semicircles at the door-steps and out in the road the wheel ruts ruled deeply in the snow.

In the morning when he awoke, the house was shrouded with stillness, and when he descended the stairs the clock had been stopped at a quarter to three and he knew that was the time when his granny must have died. He felt his jaw quivering and he looked at the closed door of the wee room, its brass handle rimmed with the light from the fire. He was afraid to go near it. His mother came in from the yard, an apron over her head to keep off the snow.

'She's gone, Frankie, poor thing. Many's a penny she gave you, and God knows the creature could ill afford it.' She dabbed her eyes with her apron. 'It was wrong to bring her from the country. It was all my fault! It was like tearing up an old bush and trying to coax it to grow again.'

He felt the tears come to his eyes and he held his head down and spent a long time lacing his boots.

'Ah, son, it's well you don't understand,' and she took his hand and led him into the wee room. A yellow blind covered the window and on the table were three lighted candles. The old woman, shrouded

170

in brown, lay stretched on the white bed, the face pale as wax and scored with wrinkles, the grey hair parted in the middle and combed around her ears.

'Kneel down, like a good boy, and say a prayer for her soul'; and while he prayed the two sisters who managed the market-stall rustled into the room and shook hands with his mother.

'I'm sorry for your trouble, Mrs. Griffin,' they said in low tones.

They knelt close to Frankie and he smelt scent off them and noticed the heels of their shoes edged with snow.

'She's not like herself, Mrs. Griffin,' one of them said.

'Ai, she's badly failed. But we're thankful to God for one thing: she got a happy death.'

'She went quickly in the end, I suppose?'

'She did. She had a lovely death.' She paused and twisted her apron. 'Hugh ran for Father Teelan. She became conscious a wee while before the last.' She paused again and sighed. 'It was the . . .'

'The children will miss her,' put in the sisters.

'They will indeed. She was always knitting for them.' Kate shook her head and looked at the corpse. She was going to say something when one of the sisters spoke.

'I suppose, Mrs. Griffin, it was a terrible break for her to leave the country?'

Suddenly Kate's face stiffened, her lips quivered, and she covered her eyes with her hand and shook her head with despair: 'Yes, yes,' she cried. 'It was . . . the city broke her . . . .'

'Ah now, Mrs. Griffin, I wish we were half as happy. She wouldn't exchange places with any of us. There's a smile on her face.'

The sisters moved into the kitchen. Kate spoke to Frankie and told him to go into Liza's for his breakfast. As he went out by the yard he saw the tracks of the dog's paws in the snow. The waste ground was white, the smoke of the dumps was blotted out, and the wind-blown snow was piled against the fence of the garden. Up from the river raced the greyhound, his nose skimming the ground; a flake of snow stuck in his nostrils and he sneezed, shook his head, and began to scrape his nose with a paw. He smelt the snow and began to dig wildly. Frankie called to him. He raised his head and dug on. Then a sparrow alighted on the topmost wire of the fence, crumbs of snow falling to the ground; and he remembered how his granny used to give him pieces of bread to throw to the birds. Two boys dragging a sheet of corrugated tin passed towards the shelving bank of the river. Without envy he watched them as they lay flat on the tin, and when their heels disappeared over the bank he went into Liza's.

Chapter XVII

On the day of the funeral the snow still fell. Peter, who had got permission to go to the funeral, was standing at the street door gazing silently at the hoof-marks on the road, the falling snowflakes, and at the sparrows hopping about on the roofs. He had grown stout; his black hair was cropped close. He wore a navy blue jersey and coat, black stockings, and new boots with stiff tabs. Behind him a bow of black crepe hung lightly from the door-knocker, and from within the kitchen he could hear Frankie asking to be allowed to go to the funeral.

'No, son, you can't go,' his mother was saying. 'You're suit's not good enough and there'd be no room for you in the motor.'

'Well, is Peter going?'

'Be a good boy, Frankie. Poor Peter is going. I'll give you something for yourself when they're all

172

away.'

He joined Peter at the door; and in silence they watched the windy snowflakes, men gathering for the funeral, and the neighbours peering out between the edges of their drawn blinds. A motor hearse and one motor came up the street, their roofs covered with snow, blue smoke clouding from their exhausts.

Johnny took the sash from the kitchen window, and the coffin was passed out to the mourners in the street. The cold snow whirled into the stuffy kitchen and fell on the brass name-plate of the yellow coffin.

'Who'll take the first lift?' Hugh said, and beckoned to Jackie McCloskey and Stick McCormick. They came forward, and presently the coffin was raised on to the shoulders of four men: Hugh and his father in front, Jackie and Stick at the back. They had no overcoats, and Stick had on black trousers, a brown coat, and white muffler. Peter walked behind carrying their caps and Jackie's hat. He saw the flakes streaking past the dark window, and in the doorway saw Eileen Curran and Liza standing with his mother and little sisters.

'Little did I think she'd be leaving this way,' cried his mother, and she dabbed her swollen eyes and watched the coffin being borne through the flickering snow out of the street.

The coffin was carried in relays of four until the main road was reached and there the glass door of the hearse was swung open to receive it. The mourners dispersed, and Johnny, Hugh, Stick, and Jackie got into the accompanying motor and Peter sat with the driver. They set off for Toome traversing the same road which Peter had taken on the wet day when he had stolen the bicycle.

'It's a tidy, respectable funeral,' Stick said, rubbing his hands and looking out of the window at the tram-lines slushed with snow.

'A lovely turn out,' Jackie McCloskey added, searching for his pipe.

Hugh sat in the corner wearing a white collar and a black tie which Eileen had bought for him. He rested his elbow on the ledge of the window, leaned his cheek on his hand, and listened in silence to the ploof of snow on the roof and to the window rattling.

'They'll charge you a good penny for this run?' Jackie queried, paring a piece of plug with his knife and coaxing the tobacco into his pipe with his little finger.

Johnny asked them to guess.

'No, you're all on the low side,' he answered them. 'I gave the undertaker her insurance policy — it's worth about twenty quid and he gave me a fiver change. He wasn't going to come at all unless he got money in advance.'

'Stiff enough,' Stick said, looking at the wet-streaked floor. 'They should have sent two motors along with the hearse for that money.'

On their fingers they began to computate the price of petrol, the mileage to Toome and back; and they came to the conclusion that the undertaker would make a profit of approximately eleven pounds. Then Hugh, without taking his elbow from the window, explained to them about the wear and tear of cars and the days on end when the undertaker would be standing with his hands in his pockets doing no business. He relapsed into silence again and saw, through a trellis of snowflakes, the moving trams. The window continued to rattle; Hugh took a piece of paper from his pocket, folded it and pressed it into the frame. The window ceased its rattling, but a freezing wind continued to circulate about the wet rubber-covered floor. Stick jigged his feet and leaned forward with his hands on his knees. The conversation turned to the merits and demerits of insurance policies, Johnny explaining how his

174

mother had been paying twopence a week for over sixty years to her burial society.

'And she only got twenty quid in the end! It's damned robbery! commented Jackie. 'Twopence a week — That's about nine bob a year. Let us say ten shillings — it'll make it easier to count. Now ten shillings a year paid out over sixty years would make a grand total of thirty pounds. And they turn round and give you a bare twenty quid. It's a damned shame!'

Stick rubbed his hands audibly: 'And, Jackie, don't forget about the interest the money has made — and every halfpenny of that goes into the pockets of the society.'

Once again Hugh looked over at them with cold contempt and pointed out to them that the old woman could have died after paying a few pence to the insurance company: 'Who'd be the loser then?' he asked them.

'Them insurance men will take damned good care that your heart's as sound as a bell before they'll put you down in their books,' replied Jackie. 'Look at me, for instance, because I have a fluttering heart no insurance man would look to the one side of me.'

Stick stamped his feet again and his eye glanced at Jackie's swimming medal dangling from its silver chain: 'I suppose it was the swimming, Jackie, that knocked the old heart up,' and he winked sideways at Hugh. They fell silent and within the motor there was no sound now except the suck-suck of Jackie's pipe and the pelt of the snow on the roof.

When they reached the end of the tram-lines the motor ran more smoothly on the country roads. Peter sat hunched up with the cold, burying his chin in his coat and feeling the pleasant warmth of his breath. The wiper swept a sector of snow from the windscreen and through this he could see the flakes swirling past the black hedges and a seam of snow on the windy side of the telegraph poles. Near Antrim the road was being mended and as the car raced by he had a glimpse of a watchman's hut, a glowing brazier, and snow lying on the handles of shovels and on upturned buckets. He wondered was it the same watchman whose cans he had flung on to the road. He shivered as a cold wind fingered his bare knees. The snow blew, head on, and time and again the driver would open the window and without stopping the car stretch out his gloved hand and scrape the snow off the windscreen. It would take a long time then before the air in the car would warm again, so Peter pulled the sleeves of his jersey over his fists and pulled his stockings above his knees, and all the time saw through the window the black twigs of the hedges, the white deserted fields, and a red cart and a horse's mane plaited with snow. He closed his eyes and fidgeted with the buttons on the upholstery of the seat, and from under three buttons picked out flakes of confetti and flicked them on to the wet floor; it was then that he observed the driver's boots and an ugly patch on the toe of one of them.

'I could put on a neater patch than that,' he said to himself, and would have liked to advise the driver on the mending and buying of boots, but the driver sat, sullen-looking, unresponsive, the collar of his coat about his ears, a dull stare in his eyes. The motor jolted over a level-crossing and he could see a deserted station and a signal stiff with snow.

'This is Toome now,' he said to the driver, 'another three miles to the graveyard at Moneyglass.'

'That's good news. I'm nearly foundered,' and the driver sat erect and straightened his glossy-peaked cap.

The country people — neighbours of the old woman — were clustered around the gate of the graveyard and Luke, the postman, came forward and shook Johnny's hand. 'I'm terribly sorry,' he said slowly. 'Terribly sorry — the road's not the same since she left. Ah, many's a cup of tea she made for me on a wintery morning.'

Johnny nodded his head: 'She broke her heart leaving.'

'I mind the day well that she took the notion to go. God be good to her, she bid me send the telegram for her.'

The bell in the little church began to ring, and they carried the coffin from the hearse through the gate of the graveyard and over a dark, trodden path in the snow. A wet slop of clay, heaped at the side of the raw grave, stained the purity of the snow. At the bottom of the grave straw floated on muddy water, and one of the gravediggers took Johnny to the side when he saw him looking down into the grave.

'We tried to teem it out this morning, Johnny,' he whispered to him, 'but it bested us. There's only about half a foot of water in it now and we covered it with straw.' But till the day he died Johnny would never forget the slap the water made when the coffin was being lowered into it.

An old priest came out to read the graveside prayers and Peter held for him in his frozen fingers the brass stoup of holy water.

'Let us pray,' he read, one hand shielding the prayer book from the falling snow. 'Almighty and most merciful Father, who knowest the weakness of our nature, bow down Thine ear in pity unto Thy servants, upon whom thou hast laid the heavy burden of sorrow. Take away out of their hearts the spirit of rebellion and teach them to see Thy good and gracious purpose working in all the trials which Thou dost send upon them. Grant that they may not languish in fruitless and unavailing grief, nor sorrow as those who have no hope, but through their tears look meekly up to Thee, the God of all consolation, through Jesus Christ Our Lord ... Amen.'

Peter watched the flakes slanting into the grave and falling with sad, mysterious silence. He could hear the seep and drip of the water from the wet mound of clay and he began to cry, and through his tears saw the mud clinging to the long-handled shovels before dropping with a hollow sound on to the coffin. He raised his head and saw the tears in his father's eyes, his misty breath, and flakes of snow on Hugh's new tie.

Johnny and Hugh took turns at shovelling clay on to the coffin and when the grave was filled in and the last piece of sod clamped back to its place they put on their caps and moved towards the gate. There a neighbour woman brought them into her house and made them tea and when they had finished Hugh and Peter crushed in beside the driver of the hearse and set off for home, leaving Johnny to loiter about the countryside and stand his friends a few drinks. The snow ceased and Johnny brought them up to the old house. The snow lay thick on the thatch and on the crossed sashes of the little windows. The air inside was bare and cold, and damp flakes of limewash had fallen on the floor. Everything was as he had left it on the days when he was down pitting the potatoes; there were tracks of a brush on the white ashes, and at the empty hearth two vacant chairs smeared with a dull light because of the cloths hooked to the windows.

Johnny took two candle butts from a drawer in the dresser and placed them on the hearthstone, and from a nook in the wall took a box of matches but failed to strike them because they were damp. Jackie handed him a box and Johnny lit the candles, stacked a few sods of turf around the flames and soon had a fire smoking up the wide chimney.

'Keep moving about, men, till the fire blazes,' he said to them. 'I'm going to the well for a bucket of water and I'll be back in a minute.'

He pushed open the wooden gate at the side of the house, cutting a black arc in the snow. He walked down through the silent field, past his pit of potatoes — white now like a child's tent. At the foot of the field the tall poplars shivered with the cold and a slush of snow covered the mouth of the well. He scooped the snow away from the bottom of the bucket and plunged it into the clear, cold water. He followed his tracks up the field to the house. The motor car was backed in off the road but he couldn't see the driver. Stick was standing at the open door of the house, stamping his feet, and keeping away from the drip of the thatch. He began to praise the house to Johnny; Johnny smiled condescendingly and thought to himself; 'A town-bred man knows nothing of the country.'

The turf was blazing and Jackie was sitting sideways to it on a chair, the melting snow dropping off his boots on to the floor.

'Man alive, Johnny, this is a grand snug, wee house,' and he puffed at his pipe, and through the open door saw the snowy hedges and above them the blue sky ribbed with bones of cloud.

'Come to you see this room,' said Johnny, and he opened the door of the room and unhooked the cloth from the window to let in more light. There was a smell of disinfectant, and a feather tick lay humped over the rail of the bed. They blew out their breaths with the cold and gazed at the cork framed picture of Robert Emmet: he was dressed in a green tunic with gold epaulettes, white tight-skin trousers, a plumed hat in his outstretched hand, the other hand gripping the hilt of his sword — below the figure a verse from 'She's Far From the Land'.

'He's the dead spit of you, Johnny, if you had

179

that moustache off,' commented Jackie.

'God have mercy on her, she used to say the same thing,' and he looked at Stick for his opinion. But Stick wasn't listening to them — he was thinking of his clutch of children and the number of partitions he'd have to make if the house belonged to him.

'Man, dear,' he mumbled to himself, 'they could run wild about them fields.'

'What's that you say?' asked Jackie.

'I was only musing — that's all,' said Stick, a little bit riled.

'Och, that make no odds. I thought you might be passing a remark about the patriot,' and he pointed with the shank of his pipe at the black cork frame.

Stick sniffed with contempt: 'I'm sure you're thinking a fat lot about our patriots! You're thinking of all the bottles them corks came out of!'

'Ai,' Jackie said, at a loss for an answer.

They went back to the kitchen. The kettle boiled and from a corner of the dresser Johnny produced a bottle of well-matured poteen. He cleaned the dust from four mugs with brown paper and made punch. He brought some to the driver who lay stretched on the seat of the car, a rug around him, his cap covering his face.

Johnny wakened him: 'There's a mug of poteen and take it slowly. There's great fire in it.' Johnny smiled to himself, for he weakened it with plenty of water knowing he had to drive them home.

Stick and Jackie were discussing the fine health they'd have if they were living in the country. Johnny laughed at them indulgently:

'It's all right for the likes of you that never wrought on the land to talk like that. There's plenty of worry attached to it — beasts dying, crops failing, and always the bad price. But I suppose it's like everything else — we must take the rough with the smooth. 'Deed it's a poor sort of a man and a

180

poor sort of a country that hasn't its uphill fights, for when a man or a country gets it easy they go to blazes.' He gave the sods of turf a prod with his boot and sent the sparks up the chimney. 'Now this place would suit a man like Jackie — he hasn't a squad of children tethered to his heels.'

'And you could have a swim every day in the Bann,' Stick said, thinking the conversation was too serious.

'All the same, Johnny, I like the city,' Jackie answered, looking at Stick and spitting contemptuously into the fire.

'And I hate it!' Johnny said firmly. 'But what can I do? The years is getting on and instead of me looking for work I'll soon be looking for work for all my children. There's not much here for any boy or girl unless you were in a big way of living and had about fifty acres of good land. I'd hate to sell this place. Och, you don't like to see your name dying out of a place where you were born and reared and where all your people is buried. I may let it for some years and maybe later on Peter or Frankie might take a notion of settling down in it.'

Johnny piled on more turf. The steam rose from their boots and trousers. The poteen made them drowsy and they dozed on the chairs till the driver knocked the door and told them that the snow might fall again and he had no chains with him for the tyres.

A reddish tint was in the sky and sparkles of frost on the snow when they set off for home again. The tyres crunched over the crust of snow. The windows rattled. The men became very cold, and Johnny thought of the thick rug that he had seen with the driver; but he hadn't the courage to ask him for it. Lights were being lit in the snowy cottages, and as they sped through a village they saw the glow of a fire in an open doorway. Jackie shivered, felt in his pockets for two half-crowns and ordered the driver to stop at the next pub.

The car stopped in the middle of a small town, but as they entered the pub a frozen chilliness came over the three of them. It was not a pub that invited you to spit or throw a spent match on the floor. The electric lights were elaborately ornate, the varnished snugs were draped with blue curtains tied at the waist, the floor was parqueted, and the shining bottles on the shelves had ruffs of coloured paper on their necks. They knew they were in the wrong establishment.

'Come on and we'll clear!' said Stick. The proprietor appeared and smiled at them expansively with gold-filled teeth: 'A cold evening, gentlemen.'

' 'Tis.'

Jackie put his pipe in his pocket and wondered would his two half-crowns be sufficient to pay for three whiskies and a stout for the driver.

'He'll spread a napkin for us on the counter,' whispered Stick.

Jackie ordered the drinks. The proprietor took down a new bottle of whiskey, lifted off its yellow ruff, stripped it to the waist, and wiped the neck of the bottle.

In silence the three of them lifted their glasses and took their whiskies in one gulp. They walked out and into the cold car again.

'That's the best ever I saw,' said Johnny.

'The country's going to hell!' from Jackie. Stick said nothing. He rested his elbow on the window ledge and stared at the lights that flew past the window, but within the core of his mind was the vision of an old pub with sawdust on the floor, a stove with a simmering jam-pot of water and evaporating spits, men laughing and sitting on barrels and throwing dead matches on the floor. The vision warmed him and when they reached home they found that he had fallen asleep. The cold frosty air wakened him. Four of his children came to meet him when they heard the car stop.

'What'd you think of the pub?' Jackie asked him before he went into the house.

Stick, his mind drowsed with sleep, looked at him with half-shut eyes: 'It was a grand place, but I didn't like the spittoons on the floor.'

'What spittoons?'

'The ones with the coloured papers round their necks,' Stick said, and walked into the house.

'I think he's drunk,' Jackie said to Johnny, 'for I seen no spittoons.'

'Nor did I.'

They separated, and when Johnny entered the kitchen he saw Eileen Curran helping Kate to clean the supper dishes. Hugh had already brought Peter back to the Home.

That night no one slept in the wee room.

Chapter XVIII

Out of the few pounds he had left after the funeral Johnny bought a second-hand bicycle for fifteen shillings, explaining to Kate how he intended to cycle on odd week-ends to the country, dig a trench or two at the back of the house to keep out the damp, divide up the room with the old partition that lay in the byre, and keep a fire going to prevent moss from settling on the thatch. In the spring time if he could get a decent price for the house and its field of three acres he might sell it.

Hugh took possession of the wee room and when he came home from the brick yard in the evenings he commenced to paper the walls, using a creamy, rose-bordered paper which Eileen had chosen for him. He carried the old woman's trunks up the stairs to the landing. He black-lacquered the fireplace, and used mahogany stain on the bare boards of the room, but the next day he had to re-stain them as the cat had got in before the stain had dried, leaving the marks of her paws on the floor. He engaged a plumber to put in gas; and when Eileen saw the lead pipe worming up the freshly papered wall and saw the smudgy blobs left by the plumber's fingers she laughed playfully : 'Hugh, you should have got the gas in before you papered the walls — where's your head! That's not the expensive kind of paper you can wash. You're too rash and you never think'

Eileen put cretonne curtains on the window and got Stick McCormick to make her a tall thin box with three shelves which she papered inside and out with a remnant of wall paper and draped the front of it with the same material as the curtains; in one shelf she would keep her polishing brushes and shoes, in another her smoothing iron, and on the top shelf her brushes and comb. And while they prepared the room in this way for their forthcoming marriage, and hung up her picture of the Holy Family above the fireplace, Eileen was also willing to help Kate with the children — washing them and putting them to bed.

'We'll get on well together,' Kate would say to her. 'And I'm glad Hugh's getting a right sensible lump of a girl.'

Kate had time to rip out some of the old woman's shawls and stockings, and with the wool she knitted jerseys for Lena and Ann, a pair of stockings for Frankie, and for Eileen's wedding present she knitted in secret a grey bed-jacket trimmed with blue satin ribbon.

At Christmas Hugh and Eileen were married quietly, and came to live in the wee room. Eileen and Kate shared between them the work of the house: Eileen did the washing and the ironing, and Kate made the dinner, using potatoes which Johnny had brought from the country. On Saturday nights

Hugh and Eileen went to the pictures or went for walks up the Springfield Road. Hugh was content and they seldom quarrelled. But in January when his mother got a few weeks' work as a weaver in one of the factories he grumbled because Eileen had to mind and wash the children, cook the meals, and clean the house.

'Eileen, I didn't think I'd let you in for all this,' he said to her one night when they had retired. 'When you were slaving for your sisters I thought our marriage would make it easier for you. And now it's this.'

'Haven't we got each other?' she laughed, and put her cold feet on his. 'Isn't the children half the day at school and half the day in bed. And as for Oliver — he's walking, and he's good company for me when you're all out. Anyway your mother's job is only to last a month or so; then things will be easier. After that your father might get a start.'

'He's been waiting for a start this past six years. He's been doing nothing but wait and wait — if he waits any longer he'll be left at the post on the Last Day. I wish he'd go and live in the country for he's half his time in it — running back and forth on that old mangle of a bike. If he did we could have this house all to ourselves.'

'Don't be selfish, Hugh!'

'I'm no selfish! I'm thinking of you all the time.'

'Well, don't lose your temper over it!'

'I'm not losing my temper. That's the thanks I get for thinking of your comfort. Good night!' and he pulled the clothes over his shoulder.

'Good night!' she answered and gave the bed a shake.

They lay quite still. Eileen put her cold feet on Hugh's again. He shrugged his shoulders and pretended to snore. A laugh from Eileen dispelled their anger and he turned and took her in his arms.

Kate had always great praise for Eileen: 'I don't

know what I'd do only for her,' she would say to Liza when she went in at nightfall to chat with her.

'She's a bit on the small side,' Liza answers with a disparaging air. 'And them high heels she wears makes her conceity-looking.'

'Och, Liza, she's not one bit proud. Wait'll you get to know her better.'

'I don't like going in near you since she came to live with you. Somehow the house feels strange. God be good to the old woman, but she had great kindness in her. But there's something about Hugh's wife I don't like. When I went to read her cup the other night she wouldn't let me. "All nonsense" she called it and turned up her nose.'

'Don't take any heed of that, Liza. She's not long married and you're too fond of ladling out sets of twins when you're reading the cups.'

'I read what's in the cups — no more, no less. I make up nothing. It's the tea-leaves that's wrong,' and Liza takes a pinch of snuff and stiffens in affronted silence. After a few shrugs from her shoulders she continues: 'The young people is all different nowadays.'

'They're the same as they always were,' Kate answers. 'It's us that's changed. When you grow older you see things different.'

' 'Deed you might be right. But all the same she makes me feel uncomfortable. I don't like the high heels and the powder on her face. And she hasn't a word to throw to a dog.'

Kate rises from the chair: 'Maybe you'll drop in the morrow night.'

'Och, Kate, come you in here — it'd be more homely. Jackie can get on well with Hugh's wife but I can't.

When Jackie came in to have a smoke with Johnny he always flattered Eileen and praised her baking: 'Man, Eileen Sweetheart, not that I should say it — but you bake better bread than Liza herself.'

186

One cold wintry night Johnny had the kitchen to himself and he gave three taps on the wall with the poker, and presently Jackie answered the signal. Johnny put on more coal, and they pulled the black sofa out from the wall and parked it in front of the fire.

'Do you know what I'm going to tell you?' says Johnny, commencing the conversation and pointing the shank of his pipe at the blazing coals. 'It's the women nowadays that keeps the fire in the grate. Kate tells me that out of her room in the factory most of them is married women and their husbands idle. It's a crying-out shame that married women with children should be out working and men wanting work and can't get it. There's Stick, next door, and I don't know under God how he keeps things going with that houseful of children. From morning to night he's always chopping sticks, whistling to himself, and skelping the youngsters.'

'Stick is a faithful client of Vincent de Paul,' Jackie says, leaning forward on the sofa, and spitting between the bars of the grate. 'Only for Vincent, he wouldn't whistle so much. But I shouldn't be talking about him — he gets on my nerves when he starts trying to be funny . . . But here's what I want to say to you,' and Jackie adopts a solemn tone. 'Take my advice and clear to hell out of this and go and live in the country. You've your own spuds and vegetables and hens and a free house.'

Johnny shook his head: 'The land's too small for us. It'd suit you and Liza if you were both drawing the old age pension. Life on the land is hard and bothersome,' he pressed the tobacco into the bowl with his forefinger. 'But I suppose our lives is all the same whether we're in the country or in the city — it's all ups and downs and discontents. I think, Jackie, there's worry in everything that has do with man. Even a man works hard he'll have

187

worry,' and he held out his hands to the heat. 'It's like this — we all get the rough with the smooth. Sooner or later a man will get his knocks; and anyone who thinks he'll sail through life like a swallow is making a hell of a mistake. Some years you get a run of luck and have a few bob in your pocket and you're as healthy as a trout, and then another year you have damn all. But surely to God there's something wrong in a world where a man has a houseful of children and he can't get anything to do but live on charity. And the worst of it is, Jackie, we can do nothing for ourselves but grouse and grumble and hope and hope. I seem to have lived on nothing else but hopes for the past six years. My life is rushing by very quick and in another ten years I'll still be hoping.'

'You'll have your children growing up around you and, maybe, a few grandchildren. They might fare better. What about Peter? I suppose he'll be out of the Home soon?'

'Easter — if he behaves himself,' said Johnny, and he plunged the poker between the bars of the grate.

'And Mary? Any word from her at all?'

'She's doing bravely, thank God, she's doing bravely. Kate gets an odd letter from her and she seems bright and happy. A good girl, Jackie, and a big loss to us,' and Johnny stared at the fire reflectively. ' 'Deed since she was no size at all she was always wanting to be with the nuns.'

As they chatted together the night grew older and they became drowsy and silent with the heat. Then Hugh and Eileen came sweeping in like a breeze. Eileen's eyes were bright, she was laughing, twirling a red felt hat in her hand, and tossing back her fair hair. On seeing the sofa pulled round to the fire she smiled: 'Leave it to the men to make themselves comfortable!' and she went into the wee room to take off her grey coat.

Jackie was on his feet when she came into the kitchen again.

'You're not going, Jackie?' she said. 'Wait for a minute or two for I'll be making a drop of tea.'

'Eileen, Sweetheart,' he smiled. 'I better be going for I have overstayed my time.'

Johnny went to the door with him. The street was dark except for the street-lamps and the light from the shop window on the opposite side. The white porcelain letters: CHOCOLATE were still printed on the window, the H and T missing, while out on the dark roadway was a reflection of the window, the word CHOCOLATE in shadowy reverse.

Behind them they could hear Hugh and Eileen laughing and joking.

'Is there anything nicer than a young married pair?' said Jackie, trying to light a spit onto the reflection on the roadway. 'They like to have the kitchen to themselves.' He walked over to the shop and Johnny leaned against the jamb of the door listening to the hard rattle of sweets being spilled into the brass scale and watching Jackie nodding his head as he spoke to the woman of the shop. Jackie crossed the road again: 'There's an ounce of plug for yourself and a few sweets for the childer.'

'I'll take the sweets but not the plug. Keep it yourself, man.'

'You've been kind to Liza and myself with your garden and the spuds you brought us from the country . . . Good night to you!' and he pressed the tabacco into Johnny's hand and went into the house.

Johnny stood at the door, cut the plug with his penknife and filled his pipe. He leaned against the jamb and puffed at his pipe with great contentment. Above the dark roof the sky was swarming with stars. From the kitchen Hugh and Eileen still laughed and he wondered what they were always laughing at. He remained at the door looking across at the light in the shop window and watching the

189

woman making white paper pokes for sweets. He blew smoke rings into the cold air, and saw upstairs being lighted. He put his hands in his pockets and jingled his few pence. Then Eileen called him for his tea, and he went in and closed the door against the cold.

Chapter XIX

Mary was the only one on the draughty platform of the station, the only one waiting for the train that was going citywards. She was dressed in black, a hand raised to her hat because it was stormy, and through her tear-filled eyes she was gazing at the railway lines and at a piece of crumpled paper being blown in the wind. At her feet lay a small suit-case — the one that her mother had carried for her on the day she had left for the convent. With pained regret she recalled every incident of that day: with her mother carrying the suit-case they had walked up the pebbled path towards the convent. White-painted stones edged the lawn, and on the loose pebbles of the path she remembered hoof-marks and a piece of caramel paper. An old gardener was pushing a lawn-mower and the grass spurted on to a sack that looped from the handle. Everything had a fresh clean smell; everything was drowsy in the warm sunshine. The vestibule door was wide open, their feet had rattled on the blackleaded door-scraper, and sun shone through coloured glass on to the brown mat. She had gently pressed the brass bell and the air was so still they heard the bell echoing through the corridors of the house. Her mother gave a nervous cough, and they listened in stiff, expectant silence and presently heard the rattle of beads, the faint rustle of a skirt, and the jingle of keys. A small lay-sister ushered them into a parlour where there was a mahogany table, a silver

190

vase of pink carnations reflecting on its polished surface. A brown butterfly had flown through the open window and they had followed it with their eyes while from outside came the hum of the lawn-mower and the thick, brooding silence of the heat. Mary sat stiff and nervous, tired with a sweet sadness. Her mother talked in whispers, continually fingering the suit-case which rested on her lap. And then when the door knob rattled again her heart jumped. She got to her feet as a little nun spoke to her cheerily, all the time twirling her girdle of rosary beads round her forefinger. Then they had tea brought to them on a tray and the little nun had slipped out quietly and they were alone again. She remembered the thickness of the cream, the white cloth and how her mother had praised the lace-design. She could eat nothing; her mother's cup rattled as she stirred her tea, and some of it jabbled on to the saucer; and she remembered how she had mopped it up with a piece of bread, her eyes on the door, and how her face had flushed. She stifled a sigh as she recalled it all.

A signal clicked and far away she heard the dim rumbling of a train. How often had she heard it lying in bed at night! How often had she denied herself the pleasure of watching the trains pass at the end of the convent fields! She lifted the suit-case and held it in front of her, gazing into the distance to where the lines converged, and there saw the twisted rolls of smoke appearing above black trees.

She got into an empty carriage and sat in the corner at the window. The train whistled and moved off. Her tears came freely, and in a few minutes she saw the red-bricked convent, a grey statue high up in the niche, and down in the fields the clothes fluttering on the lines, and below them again the black river where she had often watched the swans feeding on the green glut of seed. Though the windows of the convent were cold and cheerless she wondered if anyone were watching her train. She laughed hysterically and covered her eyes with her hand.

Going home! ... Going home! ... Going home! ... she read the words into the rhythmic rock of the wheels. What would her mother say? And then the neighbours! And Hugh's wife —now living with them! Somehow the house is not your own when a stranger comes into it!

The train rushed on and she saw the sun burst on a river, watery hoof-marks in the fields, men ploughing and gulls falling like snow about their heads. She raised her head and saw pencilled inscriptions on the ceiling; she lowered her eyes immediately and studied her hands — their thinness, the nails pale and their half-moons almost gone, the forefingers pocked with the needle. She startled as the train sped through an empty station — a ribbed, rattling sound streaking past the window.

She spread her handkerchief on her lap, twisted it, and crushed it into a ball. Her eyes ached and her hat seemed to press heavily on the back of her head. She bit her lip to keep from crying. She was told to be brave — that it was God's will.

How kind the little doctor had been when he arrived at the convent to examine her eyes! And as the various lenses had clicked into their place his voice had been gentle: Is this better? What about this? And that? And the white card with the black letters had fogged, diminished, brightened. And how she had asked him would she be able to do her work.

'Of course!' he had smiled to her. 'We'll get you glasses and that will drive away your headaches and the inflammation from the lids ... You'll need to rest your eyes for a while and then everything will be all right.' And he began to comfort her by telling her about his own daughter and how he had cured a similar weakness in her eyes. She had been happy then, but a few days later the Reverend Mother had sent for her and told her that she was not suitable, that the hard life would eventually break her health. She had broken down and cried and that night she could not sleep.

And here she was going home! God knows she had worked hard and did everything she was told to do. Told to do . . . told to do . . . told to do . . . the wheels mocked it at her as the train sped on towards the city. Tears trickled from her eyes and she clenched her fists to keep from sobbing. Telegraph wires combed past the window and then a mysterious sign 1/7 like a sum in arithmetic. She laughed for no apparent reason, and rubbed a finger along the ledge of the window and then seeing how black it had become she wiped it on her stocking. Then she saw in the distance the factory chimneys of the city and she was filled with despair. Boys were playing football in a park, trams raced along by the edge of the railway lines, people were shopping – she was back in it all again.

The train arrived. She sat on – there was no need to hurry and it so bright. If only it were dark she could sneak home without being seen.

The carriage door opened: 'Journey's end, Miss . . . want a taxi?' said a porter as he climbed into the carriage with a brush.

'No, thank you!' and she descended and stood in the dreary station. Why were stations so cold, so draughty, so dark and grey? She wouldn't go home now; she would wait until it was dark.

She deposited her bag in the left-luggage and took the first tram – an Ormeau Road – and got off at the end of the lines and walked quickly into the open country. Her shoes on the hard road sent a quivering pain to her head. Her eyes ached and she was aware of their focusing. She longed to lie down somewhere and rest – rest for hours upon end.

'What happened? . . . Sent home?' She could hear the neighbours asking her. God knows she would go

193

back again to-morrow if she were permitted.

At a stream she soaked her handkerchief and pressed it to her forehead and to her tired eyes. She took off her hat and let the cold wind embrace her hair. How heavy that hat seemed to feel! At a wooden gate she looked down across the fields to the smoking city, and turning her eyes to the left gazed into the great width of the Lagan valley with its black trees and clusters of rain-clouds piling up on the horizon. She retraced her steps and arrived at the end of the lines when the lights were being lit in the trams.

Carrying her suit-case she walked home from the station, passing through streets where she was unknown, and hurried up by the dark waste ground towards the house. The back door was open, and the gaslight from the wee room stretched out as far as the garden gate. She left her case at the fence and walked up and down along the river bank thinking of days she had seen her grandmother do the same and then recalling evenings when she herself was a little girl running to meet her father coming from the mill, taking his hand and carrying his tea-can. While she stood listening in the darkness to the flooded river she heard footsteps on the tiles of the yard and saw Hugh standing in the lighted framework of the door. The greyhound ran towards her barking; then he recognized her and licked her hands. Hugh whistled and walked out from the door.

'Who's that?' he asked.

'It's me.'

'Mary?'

' . . . sent . . . home,' and her voice broke.

'So you didn't stick it?'

She covered her eyes with her hand, and the dog ran round her in the darkness.

'There's no use standing out here in the cold,' he said to her. 'Come on into the house.' And he told her that the children were in bed, that his mother was in with Liza, and that Eileen was down with her sisters.

He closed the back door and she went into the house. The kitchen seemed smaller, the black sofa more sunken; there were the same red walls, the cage in the window, and the legs of the chest of drawers badly chipped where Oliver had hammered at them with a spoon. She left her case on the sofa and was going into the wee room to hang up her coat when Hugh stopped her.

'That's our room now,' he said.

'I forgot,' she replied timidly, and put her coat on the banisters of the stairs.

Listlessly she sat on a chair and stared at the flames in the fire. There was silence. Suddenly Hugh spoke to her and she started.

'I'll go out for my mother,' he said.

'Don't . . . not yet.'

'She'll have to know sometime!' and without waiting for an answer he went out.

She heard him rap at Liza's door. She sat erect, her hands on her lap. Her shoulders twitched nervously and she felt a cold draught blowing around her ankles. With sightless eyes she stared into the fire.

'Mary!' her mother called, Hugh remaining outside. Mary made no move. Her mother came beside her.

'Mary!' and she lifted her daughter's hands and rubbed them with her own: 'Your hands are cold, child.'

Mary's tears trickled down her cheeks, but she remained erect, her eyes on the flames of the fire.

'Mary, child, I understand. Don't fret, like a good girl. Sure we all know you done your best! Sure, child dear, that's an everyday occurrence — girls coming back from the convent. You've committed no crime,' and she patted Mary's hands and put an arm round her shoulder.

'I didn't come back! I didn't come back! They sent me back!' and she closed her eyes and shook her head.

'It was God's will, child; it was God's will.'

'Don't blame it on the Almighty!' and she put her handkerchief to her eyes and wept bitterly.

'Hush, child, hush! You're tired! Dry your eyes like a good girl and I'll make you a warm cup of tea. And you'll get into my bed to-night and get a good sleep.' And she got to her feet and with affected cheeriness began to speak of Hugh's marriage, the grand girl Eileen was, and how she had mothered the children for her when she was out at work.

And as they sat at the table Mary's mind wandered from what her mother was telling her, and her eyes stared into space and the cup shook in her hand.

That night she slept with her mother, but during the early hours of the morning she sat up and stretched out her hand to the light from the street-lamp which slanted below the blind. Her mother pretended to be asleep. She could hear her praying, then suddenly fall back in the bed, shudder from head to foot and lie still. Her mother was frightened and moved close to her to listen to the beat from her heart. Then she rose from her bed and walked down the stairs, her mother following her.

'Mary, where are you going?' she asked in a whisper.

'I want to sleep with granny in the wee room.'

'You're dreaming, Mary. Come back to bed,' and she took her by the hand, and without protest Mary went with her.

Chapter XX

By day Mary would sit at home, listless, disinclined to go out except when night had fallen. Even her appearance suffered: her hands and hair which she always kept so clean were now untidy, her coat she threw carelessly on the sofa or over the back of a chair, and when she would put it on again she would never pause to brush away the cat's hairs or smooth out the creases.

'Quit the moping and do some work!' Hugh shouted at her from time to time. But she only stared at him with wide ram-like eyes.

At night Eileen reproached him: 'Hugh, for God's sake, don't say anything to her. She'll be all right when she gets a rest.'

'She gets on my nerves the way she sits and does nothing.'

'Have patience, Hugh. She'll soon pull herself together. Mary's not the type of girl that could sit in dirt or where there's things to be cleaned. It's not in her nature to be untidy.'

'She's lazy!'

'Well, God forgive you, there's not a lazy joint in her.'

He was relieved when his father called in the doctor, and the doctor ordered a complete change for her, away from her old surroundings. Three days later Kate took Oliver and Mary to Toome where Johnny had already gone to get ready the house.

Johnny with his bicycle was at the station to meet them when the train came in. He put Oliver on the saddle and they set off to walk the two or three miles to the old house.

The air was clear — the flat, ploughed land swept by a cold wind. A dull sun was leaking through the clouds, too weak to cast a shadow from the hedges on which frilled buds were beginning to appear.

Ploughs were at the heads of fields, a wet gleam on the freshly ploughed furrows; on the brown fields withered potato-tops and weeds were raked into heaps and set alight, their blue smoke swirling a pleasant smell over the hedges. They saw the wide margins of the river Bann and the cold wind packing a jabble of waves under the banks, and in the distance above a clump of trees the old spire that was on Church Island.

'God be good to your grandmother,' said Johnny to Mary. 'But many a pilgrimage she went to that Island.'

Though it was cold Mary perspired freely. Johnny talked breezily, making faces at Oliver and teaching him how to ring the bell of the bicycle; but Mary remained silent, dragging her feet her hands limp by her sides.

When they reached the house the old woman's hens which Johnny had gathered together again, flew in panic from the wheels of the bicycle. A goat in full kid me-eh-eh-ed from the byre on hearing his footsteps. At the gable he had built a fine stack of turf and piled around it a few tree trunks and chopped wood.

There was great heat in the kitchen. A sawn tree-trunk, as thick as the body of a horse, glowed at the back of the fire giving out intense heat.

Johnny lowered the kettle which swung on the crook. Kate put mugs on the table and smiled at the brown tannin which was engrimed at the bottom of each mug. 'Johnny,' she says, 'who done the splendid washing for you when you were living on your own?'

'Myself' he said, stooping down to the fire to light his pipe. Oliver stood at the open door looking sideways at the hens and keeping his hands behind his back. Mary sat at the hearth listening to the hiss of the sap from the tree-trunk and watching the smoke rolling up the wide chimney. Kate boiled her an egg and Johnny toasted bread, and when they had finished their tea they went down before the fall of dark to visit the old woman's grave.

At first the country made no improvement on Mary. She seemed to grow more dull. She did nothing but sit at the fire, her hands on her lap, and if a neighbour called into the house she would withdraw to the room and remain there until bedtime.

Johnny often sent her to the well for water, and when he was putting in the seed potatoes he asked her to carry them out to him in a basin, and as he spread the dung he taught her to set the potatoes in a line about a hand's length apart. Her head would get dizzy from stooping and she would stand straight and feel her temples throbbing or see pinspecks of light showering before her eyes.

The days grew warmer; sparrows flew out of the byre carrying feathers and hay in their beaks; larks arose from the foot of the field and went mad with song. The goat kidded, and when Mary would be going to the well she would bring Oliver with her and coax the kid to suck his fingers. In the evenings she would go with Kate to the chapel, and coming back the night air would soothe her famished mind and with a leap of delight she would see the bright stars scattered in silver handfuls amongst the tree tops. Johnny would have the kettle on the crook when they came back and they would sit at the fire drinking tea, Mary now joining in the conversation which was usually about the old woman or about the children who were left at home in charge of Eileen. The crickets chirped and sometimes they endeavoured to walk across the hearth and Johnny would scald them with the kettle, delighted to hear Mary's voice raised in protest: 'Oh, Father, you're cruel!'

She took down the picture of Robert Emmet

and brushed away the cobwebs and dust that lay thick in the crevices of the corks. She talked about making curtains for the windows; she scrubbed the table and the dresser; she tidied the drawers, and in one of them found the letter which Johnny had written to his mother begging her to come to the city.

At Easter Peter was released from the Home and his father brought him to the country so that he could keep his eye on him. He was able to mend boots and he put a card in the window: BOOTMAKING – LOW PRICES; but it could have been an advertisement for coal — the country people taking no notice of it.

May came and the young poplar leaves at the foot of the field were varnished a light brown and shivered noisily in every breeze. The young corn, yellow green, burst through the brown soil and sucked up every sparkling shower. The hedges were snowed with hawthorn blossom and in the cool misty nights the air was thick with their scent. Peter went to the moss with his father to cut and wheel out the turf, and on wet days went to a river by himself to catch trout.

Towards the end of that month a letter came from Hugh telling them that Eileen was 'expecting', that Frankie was running wild, and that it would be selfish now to allow Eileen to be responsible for the children. That evening Mary was standing at the door, looking across the road at the leafy hedges, listening to the birds singing, and watching the setting sun stretching its long eyelashes of light between the clouds. Peter was hacking wood at the corner of the gable and beside him was a heap of last year's twigs and dry briars. Far away came the ratcheted noise of the train as it rumbled over the bridge at Toome; Mary shuddered and a sad reflectiveness brooded about her eyes.

'That clock's astray in the head, Mary,' her

mother called from the room. 'Put it right — that's the half-eight train leaving Toome.' Mary didn't hear her, and Peter leaned his hatchet against a stone, brushed his sawdusted hands on his blue jersey, and went in to fix the clock. Presently her mother joined her at the door and they set off for their usual evening walk, down to the chapel, and up to a hill on the road from where they could see the flat valley of the Bann and the mountains of Derry sinewed with the gold light of evening. Coming home again the fields were quiet around them, The cows tearing at the moist grass, the hedges crouching together in the dark companionship of night. Slowly they walked on and then Kate took Mary by the arm and squeezed it.

'Mary, child,' she said, 'I was wondering if you'd like to go home again. Of course, there's no hurry yet if you want to stay.'

'Mother,' Mary answered, 'I don't want to go back again.

'You might change your mind later on.'

'I won't. I've thought about it a long time. I'll go out to service in Ballymena or maybe get a job in one of the big houses about here.'

'Please yourself now. God knows it might be the wise thing to do if that's the way you feel,' and that night at the side of the fire when Mary, Peter, and Oliver were in bed Kate talked it over with Johnny. They read Hugh's letter again; then Johnny took the oil-lamp from the wall and placed it on the table and wrote to Hugh saying that he intended to go up at the end of the week to bring the children to the country. He put the letter in the window so that Luke, the postman, would call for it in the morning.

'We haven't much,' says Johnny to Kate. 'We'll always be living from hand to mouth — yet we'll not starve. We've good firing and a free house. I'll make another partition in the room with clean bags and it'll do till we get timbers.'

He engaged the same lorry that had taken the old
woman to the city. As they set off one sunny
afternoon the greasy driver smiled with his white
teeth and rattled away to Johnny. 'I'll never forget
that journey till the day I die,' and he would pull
at his cigarette and spit out through the window:
'This is were she made me turn!' and he laughed and
pushed his cap to the back of his head. 'She thought
she hadn't locked the door . . . I seen her doing it,
but she wouldn't believe me — indeed she would
not! . . . And this is the very spot she made me get
out and look at St. Anthony — and there he was
lying like an infant in his box of straw and the
divil the happorth up with him . . .' The lorry jabbed
in and out of pot-holes on the road; the driver
talked on. Bees struck against the windscreen. A
crude smell of grease and heat suffocated Johnny
and he held the door open to get the breeze. '. . .
And it was about here that she gripped the wheel
and nearly sent me into eternity. God have mercy
on her — she was a lively one.'

Eileen was waiting for him and had the children
washed and combed. She was pale, her eyes mild
and patient-looking. She looked smaller, because
she no longer wore her high-heeled shoes. Hugh
had two beds dismantled, ready to be hoisted on
to the lorry. His father told him he could keep
everything in the house except some of the bed-
clothes and some of the delf. Johnny decided to
take the greyhound, but offered the lark and the
cage to Hugh.

'I wouldn't have time to look after it,' Hugh said.
'Take it with you.'

'And what'd be the use of it in the country and
the birds singing at your very door? I'll go in with it
to Jackie — he'll take it.'

For a long time he talked to Liza and Jackie and
said good-bye to them a dozen times, and finally

Jackie put on a hat, called for Stick and the three of them set off to a pub to have a last drink.

When they came back everything that Johnny had intended to take with him — beds, bed clothes, and a few chairs — was stowed and tied on the back of the lorry. Frankie sat on one of the chairs and the greyhound was tied to it by a thick rope. His father made him take charge of Lena, while he took Ann and Rita in with him beside the driver. Jackie and Liza stood on the kerb to see them off; Stick was shouting and pulling at three of his children who were clinging to the back of the lorry. From their open doorway Hugh and Eileen stood together and waved their hands as the lorry roared out of the street, the dogs yelping after it. Hugh took Eileen's arm and closed the door. For some time they remained silent.

'Well, Eileen, we've the house all to ourselves.'

'We have, Hugh,' and she nodded her head, 'but it'll be lonely now with the whole lot of them gone. They were good children and no trouble.'

He put his hands in his pockets and glanced round the kitchen. 'I'm glad they didn't take the rocking-chair,' and he pressed his hands on the frayed knotted cords that criss-crossed the seat. 'I'll mend it as soon as I get good strong picture cord . . . I might be able to do something with that old sofa too. I could stuff it with flock or tow.' She nodded her head in silent assent, and he lit a cigarette and stood at the window and brushed with his hand some grains of bird-seed that lay on the ledge. The lowering sun was mellowing the red bricks of the chimneys on the houses opposite. One of the McCormicks was pushing a box-cart filled with bundles of sticks and another was knocking at the doors. Hugh inhaled the cigarette deeply and slowly puffed out the smoke.

'Do you know, Eileen, I think I'll go out and knock down the old goat's shed? — it's an eyesore.'

'Leave it alone; it might come in useful some day.'

'It'll make good firewood,' and he turned from the window and looked at her. 'Do you remember you said it was better to live week by week and not to look too far ahead?'

'Things were different then!'

'How different?'

'We weren't married — marriage changes people. We have to look far ahead now and plan.' She paused. 'In another few months, please God, you'll see your first child.'

'All the same, firewood would be useful now,' and he went out by the back and she heard him rummaging about the yard. Presently the noise of breaking wood brought her to the door. He was knocking down the shed, and as he belted at the roof from the inside the stones on the top bounced off it. 'Hugh!' she called to him, but he didn't hear her. She walked carefully up the yard again, and though the air was mild she went into the house and put on her coat. When she came out again he was standing on the old handcart levering up the roof of the shed and already a pile of broken wood lay at his feet.

'We'll have as much firewood as'll do us to Christmas,' he laughed, the dust covering his black hair, the butt end of a cigarette smouldering amongst the weeds of the garden.

'Don't knock it down,' she pleaded. 'It's nice to sit and lean against it on a sunny day.'

'Can't you sit at the back door? — sure there's no difference,' and he prised up a roof-board with the claws of the hammer and tore at the felt.

For some reason she was too weary to restrain him, to argue with him, and she retraced her steps and stood at the back door gazing at the river and the smoke rising from the dumps. There was great stillness in the evening, the river reflecting the gold light of the sky. Then she heard the ugly snort of the suction-pump in the brick yard, and as she listened to its foreboding sound it grew more penetrating until there seemed to be no other sounds except it and the hammerings of Hugh. 'What would he do if the brick yard closed down?' she asked herself, and before she had time to answer, Hugh called to her holding out in the palm of his hand a delicate moth which was shedding its chrysalis. 'There's a few more in the corner of the shed,' he said.

'Well, put that one back with the rest. To-morrow might be another warm day,' and she went into the house, and Hugh remained chopping at the boards till she called him for his supper.

It was getting dark, and he pulled down the blind but did not light the gas. They sat at the fire, the cups resting on their laps. Eileen was subdued, silent, and he noticed tears in her eyes.

'What's wrong with you at all?' he asked her.

'I don't know, Hugh, I don't know . . . I'm just weary.' At that moment Jackie McCloskey came up the street singing: 'Fare thee well for I must leave thee'; he stumbled against the window-sill and Liza pulled him into the house. There was silence. Then Eileen started as something heavy fell on to the tiles of the yard, and Hugh went out to pick up the boot-last which he had lent to Jackie a few days ago.

'Look here, Eileen,' he said, holding the boot-last in his hand, 'don't ever lend anything to Liza. That idiot of a husband doesn't know how to behave himself when he's drunk and he'd fling everything you lend her over the yard-wall. I'm telling you there'll be quare changes in this house from now on. We'll make our own friends. My mother had them spoiled.' He put the last below the sofa. 'I must start on that sofa soon before you fall through it. And there's that red wall gets on my nerves. We must paper it . . . You're not listening to me at all.

Eileen, what are you thinking about?'

'Och, Hugh,' she sighed. 'I'm thinking of the children in that old lorry — will they arrive safe?'

'Is that all?' and he shook his head. 'Of course they'll arrive safe! It's only about thirty miles and the roads is good.' He put his arm around her and kissed her, and with closed lips she smiled back at him.

'Don't worry, Eileen, they'll be all right. Go to bed now and get a good sleep.

In bed she lay awake for a long time thinking about the children in that ramshackle of a lorry, and in the morning she watched at the window for the postman. For a whole week she watched, and at the end of the following week the postman handed her a letter. She opened it and sat down to read it on the sunken sofa:

'Dear Eileen,

'I should have dropped you a line before this to tell you how the children is getting on in their new home. It's like yesterday since they jumped off the lorry like hens out of a basket. Poor Ann was as sick as a dog over the smell of the engine and she was in bed for three full days but she's all right again and is able to touch food thank God. The weather is good and Johnny has his spuds in and has some seed left over that'd do Hugh for the wee garden if he wants them let me know. Take care of yourself like a good girl and the children is praying for you every night and I'll send you a holy medal for yourself later on when I get things settled up. Don't worry child God is good. Don't stretch and be hanging up curtains. Hugh's a bit headstrong but take the easy way with him. If you see any bargains in the market let me know. You'd know the kind of thing that'd be in my line — boys' pants and coats and men's trousers. Johnny's very hard on trousers and I'm never done patching. You'll be glad to hear that Mary has a nice kind of mistress in Ballymena. She is not one of our sort and she plays the harmonium all day on Sunday and had twenty-three girls in singing and Mary had to make tea for them all and wash twenty-five cups. You'd wonder where one house'd get so many cups but I suppose people in a big way of living don't know what to do with their money. Peter has a bootmaking card in the window but he might as well have a bit of fly-paper. The master was glad to get our children for his school and he left Peter in his boots to sole but he hasn't paid him yet for he said he'd leave in another pair and pay for them all on the bat. But all masters is honest and that's nearly a week ago and they say he's fond of a wee drop. God forgive me if I'm taking away his character and leather the price it is. He put heels on the sergeant's shoes but you know the big size of feet they have and Peter had a penny profit. But it's better than nothing and the country people mend their own. The people's more curious here than at home. They like to know your business and they're very close and don't tell you much of theirs. You'll take a run down some Sunday in August and the change will do you good. Tell Liza we were asking for them. They're nice neighbours and I'll never forget Liza's kindness when the old woman was bad. It's only when you're down in the world that you know good friends, fair weather friends is no good. The dog caught a few rabbits in the demesne. That's all at present and you'll write soon and let me know how yous is all doing.

Eileen read the letter twice and put it in her blouse. She went to the back door and looked across the waste ground to the brick yard. She no longer heard the snort of the suction-pump or saw the ragged gap left by the demolished goat's shed. The white cat came out of the dishevelled garden and climbed on to her shoulder. She stroked it and felt its warm, contented purr against her cheek. She waited until she saw Hugh wheeling his barrow towards the drying shed. She waved to him, and pushing his barrow with one hand he waved back. She smiled and looked up the waste ground to where little girls were gathering in a ring to play some kind of a game.